High .... for
CHAMPAGNE & COCAINE
by Richard Vetere

"Vetere captures the decadent 1980s just as the iconic decade leaves the starting gate. His lead character Danny Ferraro is a deer in the headlights blinded by the lure of depravity, the mob, drug-induced sex and the gaudy glamour of the night club scene. Vetere's page-turning *Champagne and Cocaine* oozes vibrancy, written by an author who knew New York City at that time well enough to put his own stamp on its origins."
—JUDGE EDWIN TORRES, author, *Carlito's Way* and *Q&A*

"Evocative and gritty as only New York can be, Richard Vetere's *Champagne and Cocaine* is testimony that intelligent men spiraling through destructive choices can make for a hell of a read. Calculation is for the poker tables in Vetere's backroom world of early-'80s mobsters. The rest of the time, it's all about grabbing the good stuff, in quantity. So do as they do: read the book, enjoy the ride, and bury the evidence later."
—ROBERT H. PATTON, author, *Patriot Pirates* and *Cajun Waltz*

"I devoured it."
—TONY DANZA, actor

"Neighborhood friendships mixed with blow and bubbly throw Danny Ferraro into scenarios that make for good drama. More than a novel, *Champagne and Cocaine* is a smooth read, a meditation on the dangers of mixing reality with art in New York's disco era. Ferraro is one of Vetere's greatest characters, a man with ideals who has the soul of a writer, and the wardrobe of a punk. When the real keeps getting in his way he relies on poker logic and street smarts to survive even when he loses more than money."
—FRED GARDAPHE, author, *From Wiseguys to Wise Men*

Champagne
and
Cocaine

Champagne and Cocaine

A NOVEL

Richard Vetere

THREE ROOMS PRESS

New York, NY

Champagne and Cocaine
A NOVEL BY
Richard Vetere

ISBN 978-1-941110-29-4 (print)
ISBN 978-1-941110-30-0 (ebook)
Library of Congress Control Number: 2015955345

COVER AND INTERIOR DESIGN:
KG Design International
www.katgeorges.com

DISTRIBUTED BY:
PGW/Perseus
www.pgw.com

Three Rooms Press
New York, NY
www.threeroomspress.com
info@threeroomspress.com

Champagne
and
Cocaine

NEW YORK CITY

LATE WINTER, 1980

1

I SAT IN MY SEVENTY-SIX GREEN Pinto, the model that was found to have an exploding gas tank, in the parking lot of a cheap motel across from Astoria Park under the Triborough Bridge.

It wasn't ten yet and the night air still had a residue of winter chill but all the snow had already melted. I was a little early and glad I was. I turned down hanging out with some guys in the city so I could be at the game on time.

I sat back behind the wheel feeling around for a comfortable place in the worn-out seat and thought about the news of the day. I heard on the radio that President Carter decided the US would boycott the Summer Olympics in Moscow. It made me feel bad for the athletes.

And the *Post* ran a story about the mob guy, Angelo Bruno, who was shot dead in Philly a few weeks ago. He was sitting in his car at night just like I was, except he was in front of his house. Somebody put a shotgun to his head and blew a hole through it.

They had just found his body in a trunk in New York. Not far from where I was sitting and they stuffed three hundred-dollar bills up his ass and three more down his throat. Whoever whacked him was making a statement that the aging Bruno had been greedy.

I wasn't greedy. I just wanted to win. Since I left my job at Monsignor McClancy High School at the end of last semester I lost my weekly paycheck. But I was doing okay these last few months. I was winning nice and steady.

I liked teaching English but the long hours were taking away from my poker playing nights and most mornings I had a real hard time getting to my early classes in Jackson Heights. Lately, however, I could win more in one pot than the city paid me in one month and more free time gave me the opportunity to finish my novel.

Though, I liked teaching the kids and enjoyed explaining the brilliance of Faulkner and Fitzgerald. Of course, my motley class of working-class kids couldn't care less. But to them I was cool since when I was talking to them about books and literature I was talking poker and they loved it.

The students I would miss—the principal and the administrators could kiss my ass. So what if I couldn't get myself to class on time. What teenager wants to hear about grammar at nine a.m.? I was a night owl and you played poker, the real poker, *after* dark.

I wasn't sure exactly who would be at the game but I knew they were big bettors and high rollers and there would be a pile of cash to be made.

Before I left the car I placed a crisp twenty-dollar bill in the glove compartment for good luck.

2

THE GAME WAS FIVE-CARD STUD NO-LIMIT poker. I had been dealt a pair of aces as hole cards: the ace of spades and the ace of clubs. My one face-up card was a five of spades.

I looked around the table. The ante was two hundred and I had my last remaining five grand in front of me in blue and green. I was already down a grand thanks to being constantly dealt the second-best hand.

In five-card stud poker you play your best five cards. It's even that way if you play seven-card poker. It's always the best five cards. Our game had no "wild" cards, no high–low. Our game was simple: the best hand meant the best five cards you held.

There's a saying in poker that if you look around the table and you can't find the sucker, it's probably you. I spent the last seven hours looking around the room and I was sure it wasn't me. In fact, there were a handful of "suckers" at the table.

Louie "Bug" with big pale blue bug eyes was down two grand mostly because he played aggressive and stupid. Jimmy "Chaps" who always wore heavy cologne was already down the same and was playing just as wild and reckless. The black guy from Jamaica, Hilly, was down a grand because of bad cards, and Sully—all three hundred pounds of polished white flesh of him—was down a few hundred playing everything close to the vest. Only Charlie, Charlie Durrico, was the winner, the big winner.

I glanced around the room as everyone was looking over their cards. The bottles of scotch, vodka, gin and whiskey were all nearly empty. The ice bucket was nothing now but melted ice and the ashtrays were filled.

Most in the room were doing lines of cocaine that Durrico sold at a fair price. I resisted. I never liked getting high when I played poker. I had a few sips of my scotch and water some five hours earlier and now it laid in the plastic cup looking the color of urine.

"Your move, Danny," Hilly said, helping me to focus. I looked around the table again. Everyone had checked so I raised. I bet two hundred and watched to see who stayed in.

Only Sully called, leaving Durrico to bet. He looked at me and smiled. "I raise. Two hundred more," he said.

He had a king of spades in front of him so I took him for a pair of kings. Sully went out and I called. I thought I could raise again but I stopped myself.

Jimmy was dealing and my next card was the nine of spades. Durrico got a five of spades. I was still ahead in my thinking so I bet four hundred. Durrico paused and called.

I had to figure him for kings now. I figured he called because that's the way winners sometimes are. They are on a streak so they call everything figuring they're going to hit it. He must have figured he'd pull a third king or another pair. He looked at me a bit puzzled, figuring me no doubt for a big pair. No way could he figure me for a pair of aces.

Jimmy dealt. We played five-card stud with the last card up so I waited and saw that my next card was an ace of hearts. I had trips now. I had three aces and I had to have Durrico dead to rights. I barely glanced at his last card. It was a three of spades.

So there I was with three aces facing Durrico's three of spades, ten of spades and king of spades. I looked at Durrico and bet. "All in."

He looked at me, his large dark eyes focused on mine. He was a couple of years older than me but it was easy to see that he lived hard. His skin was rough from years of cigarette smoking and scotch on the rocks and very little sleep. He wore a fine white linen shirt more expensive than my entire wardrobe, which consisted of a sports jacket and slacks with a short-sleeved black shirt.

Though we had been in the room for hours the shirt still looked clean and ironed and his thick wavy black hair was perfectly coiffed.

"I raise," he told me. "Ten grand. Ten grand more to see my hole cards."

I was thrilled but I was short. "I only have my five grand," I said. "I thought we were playing table stakes?"

He half grinned. "You're good for it, no?"

I was quiet. I looked his cards over. He had three spades. I had three spades myself. There were only seven left in the deck. Did he actually have two more? This was a big-time bluff and anyway, how could I lay down three aces in five-card stud?

"What a bluff, man," Mickey Delarosa said.

"Nice, Charlie, nice," Hilly shot in.

I glanced to the window where the guys put up a bed sheet to keep out the light. The motel room was small and I felt it getting smaller. I forgot what day of the week it was.

"Ten grand more?" I asked. So that was it. I could make a big deal of it and say he had to match my all in and call it a hand but if I was right, I could make a big pay off.

If he *had* the flush I would be down my six grand *and* ten more. I had nothing in the bank. Nothing. Plus I'd owe Charlie Durrico ten grand. How could he have the flush? It *was* a big moment to pull off a great bluff.

I moved in my chair. I reached for my scotch and downed what was left in the glass. I looked back at Durrico. He hadn't moved a muscle in his face. I eyed his gold watch, his gold pinky ring and his manicured fingernails. I couldn't lay down three aces. Sometimes life is like that; you *can't* throw away a great hand even if you are second best. I nodded. "Call."

He turned over his hole cards: the nine and ten of *spades*.

My stomach dropped. The guys cheered Durrico but he was quiet and smirked. He nodded to me to turn over my hole cards. I did. He saw the aces. "Bad luck," he said without inflection.

I got up. "When do you want the money?"

"By next Sunday," he said, taking a glassine envelope out and pouring a line of coke on the table. "Take a hit, you need it." I reached for my jacket pocket that hung over my chair and pulled out my own straw. I snorted the entire line. I raised my head. I felt white heat blast through my sinuses into my brain cavity. I lurched back. The cocaine blew the cobwebs out of my skull but it didn't help with the sting of losing ten grand in one call.

I walked to the door, opened it and quickly left.

Once outside my brain was blasted again, this time with morning sunlight. I fell against the wall and took a breath. I walked to my car, got in and found my sunglasses on the passenger seat and drove home listening to morning radio trying not to remember I owed Durrico ten grand with one week to pay. I fought morning traffic and people on their way to work on my way home to sleep. Some guy on the radio was talking about how much Americans had reason to be proud of our Miracle On Ice Hockey team. "That was a month ago!" I said to no one in particular and shut off the radio. For some reason I opened my glove compartment and found the crisp twenty-dollar bill I left there *for good luck.*

When I got home, I took the elevator up to my sixth floor apartment, got undressed, found my earplugs and got into bed. All I wanted was silence.

* * *

LOU SANTUCCI WAS MY OLDEST FRIEND. I grew up in his house until I was five years old. My grandmother and his mother were friends back in Williamsburg, Brooklyn, since the forties. Lou's mother was once voted Queen of the Italian Feast of Our Lady of Mount Carmel and stood on the platform on North Eight Street waving to the crowd; now she looked like any woman would who ate what she wanted and smoked day and night for the last thirty years. My grandmother died twenty years earlier but our families had that bond created decades ago so I could go to Lou for anything and feel like family.

I met Lou in his office on Meeker Avenue around five. He had a small office but a huge business. He sold heavy construction machinery including bulldozers, earthmovers, dump trucks and steamrollers to companies all over the world. He inherited his father's business and turned a small-time mechanic shop into an international gold mine. He had a brain for money and people. He also had a knack for real estate. He believed in Long Island City but that wasn't taking off. He did invest around his office in Williamsburg and Greenpoint, Brooklyn.

It was already dark. I had spent the day doing all I could to sleep. I went in and out of my dreams haunted by the image of a nine and ten of spades. I was fatigued when I met with Lou.

I could hear "Refugee" playing on his little transistor radio sitting on his desk. Lou was humming along off-key just how he always liked to do but I don't think he realized he was humming off-key.

Lou was my height but twenty pounds overweight with a baby face and bad complexion. He had milky brown eyes and thick curly dark hair. "Bad luck, Danny boy," he said shutting off the radio.

"I played *my* cards, not his. My mistake."

"You turned into a degenerate gambler. I never met a gambler who had a dime to his name," he said. His voice was always at an even keel. He never lost his temper that I had ever seen. In front of him was a mound of paperwork and cash, mostly twenties, and I counted a few thousand dollars of it. "Why didn't you stick to the teaching?"

"No *rush* in it."

"Yeah, but you were good at it."

"I'm writing a book."

"Oh, yeah?" he said, looking at his cash then me. "Looking to sell it as a mini-series? That's what they do today, no?"

"It's about my grandfather Mike," I said.

"He was a degenerate gambler, too," Lou shot back.

"He killed that Nazi on the Brooklyn docks in forty-two," I defended.

"True," Lou agreed.

I focused my eyes on his, which wasn't easy to do since Lou never looked anyone in the eyes unless he was angry. "I came to you for a loan."

Lou stopped what he was doing. "I know why you're here. Of course I'll help you out."

I took a deep breath.

"You will catch a beating if you don't give him the full ten grand, you know that."

I didn't.

"But you have to give him something. You got collateral for me?"

I shook my head. Lou's office was small, cluttered, and worse than that, without a window. Lou drank Coca-Cola all day and loved his occasional hit of cocaine like everyone else.

"I don't have anything, Lou."

He sat back in his chair and stared for a moment at a half-eaten salami and cheese sandwich. "Tell you what, you can work it off for me."

I nodded. "Doing what?"

"Whatever. Drive for me. Drop stuff off. That kind of thing."

"Okay," I said.

"I can give you two grand right now. You give this to Durrico next Sunday. Tell him more is on the way. He's a cocksucker but he will know it came from me. He'll like that."

I nodded.

Lou pulled a locked metal box out of the top drawer of his metal desk and pulled two grand in twenties and fifties from an envelope inside.

"Durrico sucks. I hate the bastard but you're my friend. I have to stand up for you. He knows that."

"Why do you hate him?" I asked.

Lou shrugged. "Business shit we did in the past never worked out because he was always fucking me over something."

I stood there feeling stupid. Here I was, the guy who went to college, the guy who had a degree in education, asking the uneducated half-a-wise-guy family friend to bail my ass out of a jam. I could sense Lou was enjoying every minute of my humbling experience.

"Here's the two grand. Give it to him Sunday. All of it. It might save you from a broken arm."

I took the cash and tried my best to stick it in my wallet, but it didn't fit so I put it in all four pockets of my pants and jacket.

"So, you start working for me tonight."

"Sure," I said.

"I need you to go to the airport around nine to pick up Rebecca," he said.

"Who's she?"

"My new *thing*, man. She's from Islip originally and now she lives in Tampa. Gorgeous. I'm putting her up in this apartment I just got over on Twenty-First and Lex. Pick her up at La Guardia and take her to this address."

He wrote down an address on a piece of paper and handed it to me.

"Use the Lincoln. I'll leave it outside the gate."

As I turned he called me. I walked back to his cluttered desk and he handed me a white envelope. "Use a little yourself but give most of it to her. And call me once you drop her off."

The two grand felt like dumbbells in my pockets. I knew of a game over at a country club in Malba. I looked at my watch and figured I'd have a few hours to make a few bucks. I drove like a maniac, got into the game they ran in the recreation room in the back. It was a hundred dollar buy-in seven-card poker, played mostly by retired guys who'd rather lose their money than listen to the wife with the stiff dyed hair and wrinkled face complain.

I played for a couple of hours and was hitting everything: inside straights, trips, flushes and full house beating out another full house. It was 8:30 p.m. and I was up nearly seven hundred when I had to excuse myself and run over to LaGuardia. It was the kind of night I wish I had playing Durrico.

* * *

REBECCA'S PLANE GOT IN EARLY AT La Guardia but I was close and was there a few minutes later. She was making a face when I walked up to her at the baggage bin. Lou must have described me because she knew who I was twenty feet away. She was pissed, as if she was waiting for a parade and there was none for her. "This is how he treats me?" she said.

I apologized and carried her bags to the car. She got in the back seat and pouted. I checked her out in the rearview mirror and found she was checking me out.

Right off the bat I could see why Lou was stuck. She was pretty *and* sexy—like a full house in a five-card stud game. She had a heart-shaped face with dimples. Her eyes were light colored, though I couldn't see if they were blue or brown. I figured them to be hazel. She did her makeup just right with streamlined eyebrows. Her lips were full and inviting though she was looking at me like I was some peon and she was Marie Antoinette.

I drove along the Parkway and took the Midtown Tunnel into the city. Somewhere in the tunnel she spoke up. "You got anything for me?"

I had forgotten about the cocaine. I reached into my pocket, turned and handed it over to her. She took it and snorted a quick hit. She nodded to herself and smiled at me.

I focused on driving. When we pulled up to the address she wouldn't get out. "Lou said there'd be a doorman. I'm not getting out if there isn't a doorman."

I didn't say anything. I sat back and waited.

"Lou said you were from Tampa," I said.

She sat back and seemingly relaxed. "Originally Islip, but we moved when I was a kid down to Miami and then all over Florida. I hated Islip."

I turned the rearview mirror around so I could get a better look. She had soft features despite her attitude. Her eyes were light blue, her hair brown and now I could see that her makeup was a little overdone. She had a friendly, beautiful face that made you think she was the girl next door that should have been born in a palace, and there was something more. The something more being that she was probably into rough sex, maybe switching up between being the submissive and the dominant one. I was probably totally wrong but that was what I got when I took a look at her face. She was delicious but dangerous.

"How long you know Lou?" she asked, her voice softer now.

"My whole life. We grew up together."

"And you drive for him?" she shot back.

"Tonight I do," I said when a doorman appeared. "There he is."

She quickly got out of the car without saying a word, took a step toward the doorman and stopped. She came back to the car and tapped on the door. "My bags," she said sharply.

I jumped up and opened the trunk, taking the bags and handing them to the doorman.

"You're not very good at this," she said, handing me the white envelope as a tip. I watched her walk into the building and drove off.

I quickly found a pay phone two blocks east and called Lou. He told me to come by his house by midnight and pick him up. With a few hours to kill I raced back to the game in Malba, did a hit of the coke, won another two hundred, drove to Lou's mini-mansion and waited for all the lights to go out.

In minutes he was at the car. "I'll drive he said." I slid over and he got behind the wheel.

"I had to give the wife a sleeping pill and a half to knock her out. She's getting used to them. How was Rebecca?"

"Good," I answered.

"I met her down in Miami buying some machinery. She was in this club. The hottest chick in a room filled with hot chicks. She's cool about the wife so far. But she costs. These women really get me. Here she is telling me she was a school-teacher, like you, then the next thing you know she's an escort. They all got an angle, these broads. I bought her some nice jewelry, I pay for her car down there in Tampa, I lease it for her and now I fly her up here and put her up for a few weeks just so I can hit that ass and get a blow job."

"She's hot, though, Lou."

"That she is. I love the tits and how she does her hair. It flows nice, you know. Nice."

When we got to the East Side Lou jumped out of the car. "Pick me up around 2:30 a.m."

I watched as Lou entered the apartment building and I had to admit I was jealous. Rebecca was the kind of woman a guy who looked like Lou would have to pay for.

I suddenly felt a wave of sleep come over me. I gave into it. The car was comfortable and I needed rest.

I was in a deep sleep when Lou came to the car and nudged me. I woke up, slid over and he got behind the wheel. He drove off humming to himself. He always liked to hum to himself when he was in a good mood.

"I really like this one," he said.

I listened.

"She's got style, you know? Style and class. Hard to put that aside. She had everything nice up there. She had a bottle of Moët delivered for us. I paid for it, of course, and some caviar and some nice Marvin Gaye playing," he said, thinking to himself. "I have to get the wife out of town somehow." He turned to me. "You want some coffee?"

We stopped at Sarge's, the all-night deli on Third Avenue, and had some. I was half asleep eyeing the nighthawks who were eyeing me and Lou back.

On the drive through the Midtown Tunnel Lou continued to hum. Out of the blue I said, "Not all girls are like Rebecca."

Without missing a beat he said, "Sure they are. Even my wife. They all have a price."

For some inane reason he started humming "YMCA" and looked out the window.

When we got to his house, he handed me two hundred-dollar bills and got out. "Visage tomorrow night. Get some rest. It's going to be champagne and cocaine all night."

I went home to sleep and put the two hundred inside the pages of my novel *Loon Lake* on the shelf. Then didn't move for nearly ten hours.

3

THE VISAGE CLUB WAS A THREE-STORY building on Fifty-Sixth Street between Ninth and Tenth Avenues, which was in the middle of nowhere. I had gone to dinner with Lou and Rebecca over at Chow's on Fifty-Seventh on the East Side and now drove cross-town to the pits of the West Side.

Studio 54 had just closed its doors for good. When it came to clubs in New York City it got all the press but none of the people I hung out with liked it. Lou and Durrico wouldn't go near the place because you had to wait on a line at the front door to get picked to be let in. We went to Visage.

Some of the streetlights were out and nobody lived around there. The place was called Hell's Kitchen since it was mostly made up of old tenements. As I drove west the world seemingly got darker, as it always did on the West Side. When we reached Tenth Avenue, we found a couple of homeless guys who were acting as valet parkers.

I drove up alongside them and handed them five bucks each. "Watch the car and there's more for you when we get out," I said to them. I knew that if you didn't tip them they would smash the window of your car and take out the radio.

Looking sexy and leading the way, was Rebecca in a very tight silver skirt and black heels, with Lou slightly behind her in black slacks and an expensive dark blue jacket. I was tailing them both like a bodyguard, which by my looks was far from the truth.

Rebecca had her toenails painted a dark red and even her toes looked perfectly aligned. She had the shape of a 1950s Playboy Bunny and had no problem letting people know.

Lou paid the twenty-dollar entry fee each for all of us, and as soon as we walked over a red carpet and the doorman opened the large glass doors, we were bathed in light and "I Love the Night Life" was playing as if on cue.

Visage was a combination of Vegas casino and three-ring circus. A large swimming pool hung from the first floor ceiling where a nearly nude young couple swam through the crystal clear water. Waitresses wore light blue-gray dresses cut high above their knees so when they bent down or walked up the stairs the patrons got a clear view of their thighs exposing their ass cheeks. Most of the waitresses were eager for tips so they wore thin thongs or no underwear at all. Most of them were struggling actresses, college students, or just pretty girls who came to the Big Apple in the hope of being discovered or marrying a sugar daddy who was as handsome as his bank account was limitless. I was always surprised how well they balanced trays and glasses while walking up and down stairs all night, exhausted and sometimes stoned.

Lou and the guys I knew all preferred the large bar on the second floor so we walked up through the multi-colored flashing lights as our senses were bombarded and the rooms were filled with the music of Blondie, Queen and Michael Jackson.

As we reached the top of the stairs "Funkytown" by Lipps Inc was playing. The DJ blasted the songs out, feeding our collective need to get down on the dance floor.

It wasn't long before the three of us were at the bar when Lou raised his hand and in minutes a bottle of Moët champagne was brought over by one of the pretty waitresses who filled our long stem glasses. Lou paid cash on the spot along with a nice tip. Moët went for a hundred dollars a bottle.

I watched Rebecca sip her champagne eyeing the crowd looking at what the other girls were wearing. She was pretty and belonged in the spotlight. Lou couldn't take his eyes off of her, doing all he could to amuse her, get her attention, show her off. He also had a vial of coke and kept handing it to Rebecca who waved him off a few times but I knew what she was doing. She was waiting for a buzz from the champagne. She was waiting for the exact moment when the buzz from the booze made its way to her brain, and as it did, slowly peeled away her defenses. She was waiting for that exact moment when the booze couldn't take her any further and that's when she would do a line, allowing the coke to blast its way through her brain cells, shooting her off into the stratosphere where there was no turning back.

I saw the look on her face when that moment came. Lou pulled the coke from his pocket and handed it to her. She palmed the vial and disappeared into the ladies room.

"Nice, huh?" he mumbled.

"She is."

"I'm digging her, man."

"I see it," I said.

"Big time, I got feelings for her. Big time," he went on.

That was about when Durrico made his entrance. He had four women with him and two guys. He walked over and Lou stood up and hugged him. Durrico looked at me and nodded. "Sunday," was all he said.

Lou didn't say a word about me to Durrico. I was hoping he would but he didn't even glance at me.

Several waitresses came over with tiny chairs for us to sit on. Durrico's people stood around the table.

"I have some of what I owe for you," I told him.

"*Some?*" He grinned. He eyed Lou. "Tell your friend I want it all."

"He knows he owes you," Lou said, his voice stern but not tense.

"You can talk to me, Charlie, I'm right here," I said calmly.

Durrico seemed pleased with my speaking up.

"You want a bottle?" Durrico asked Lou.

"Have of some of mine," Lou answered.

Just then Rebecca emerged from the ladies' room and made her way to our table as "Ride Like the Wind" came blasting through the speakers. I watched as she glided to our table and sat down next to Lou who immediately put his arm around her.

Durrico took notice of Rebecca the minute she emerged from the ladies' room and now she was squeezed in between Lou and him.

"I don't drink Moët," Durrico said, eyeing Rebecca and ignoring Lou. "Moët is for those with no taste. I like Mumm. What about you?" he asked Rebecca.

"I love Mumm," she answered.

I could see Lou's brow tighten.

I wasn't the only one there who knew that no one at the table could tell one champagne from another if they were tasting it blindfolded.

Durrico flagged a waitress. "Do my friend here a favor, sweetie, and bring over three bottles of Mumm on me. Serve the Moët to the busboys," he said, handing her a wad of cash as a tip.

"You don't drink Moët now?" Lou chided Rebecca.

"I never liked it," she shot at him, turning up her nose.

"Is this your girl?" Durrico asked.

Lou jumped in. "Yeah, why?"

"I didn't mean to start anything, Lou. Drink your Moët if you want," he said.

"I'll take your Mumm," Lou stated. "Do you want my coke, Charlie, or do you have a preference on where it comes from?"

Durrico grinned. "Colombians make the best cocaine."

"The poppy comes from Afghanistan," I said.

Before anyone could say anything, three waitresses appeared flying through the crowd carrying bottles of Mumm on trays, along with another tray of long stem glasses.

Durrico paid them all with wads of cash, giving me a sly glance as if to say, *this is your cash I'm spending.*

I wasn't comfortable. I was watching one of his entourage eyeing me. A tall guy they all called Wack. Wack kept grinning at me, making me feel very uneasy.

A girl in a white dress spoke up. "I love Tattinger," she said.

"Tattinger is piss," Rebecca said loudly, making sure Durrico and Lou heard her and also making sure that if she was Durrico's girl everyone knew she had no sophistication.

"I can make an exception for Dom Pérignon," Durrico said directly to Rebecca as if the words themselves were the ultimate in seduction.

"A man should drink Dom Pérignon," Rebecca said soulfully.

Lou was now taking a stance physically and I thought for sure there were going to be fists flying any second.

"Your girl knows her champagnes," Durrico said. "Lou, you have great taste in everything, champagne and women and cars and friends," Durrico said lifting his glass to Lou.

Lou backed off and didn't raise his glass.

It was then this guy called Lenny "The Roach" stepped up to us, easing the tension. He was a Colombian with a big-time connection to a Puerto Rican dealer, Eddie, in the Bronx, who provided the cocaine Lou and Durrico bought.

"The Roach" was dressed in a flashy white jacket and black slacks and you could smell his cologne a mile away. He was flanked by two other guys. One looked mean and nasty with a deep black beard and wavy hair. He spoke only Spanish to Lenny and I figured him to be the muscle.

Lenny took both Lou and Durrico aside to talk business away from everyone else and Rebecca found herself being ignored.

I had heard that Durrico was looking to expand into the Bronx and partner up with Lenny. Lou thought the idea was insane.

"You don't partner up with a Colombian," he said to me an earlier night at Visage. "If they don't like you for some reason, if they think you fucked them over, even if they don't have proof but they think you did, they cut your head off and leave it in the street. Durrico is asking for trouble if you ask me."

The other guy with Lenny "The Roach" was really odd-looking. He was known only as the Swede. He was very slight, with stringing light brown hair and long silly looking whiskers from his ears to his chin.

"You want to buy a .45?" he asked me. He was always looking to sell something.

"No thanks, Swede," I said.

"I got a couple new TVs just come in," he said. He edged closer to me. I could see three women standing behind him. Lenny "The Roach" ordered a bottle of Moët for them and they were now sitting at the bar. As Lenny shook hands with Durrico, Lou and the girls were smiling and trying to get our attention. The two were gorgeous Colombian ladies wearing loose colorful skirts and the most fashionable shoes. The other lady was in white with long red hair. She was the one Rebecca dished moments ago and was now being quiet and looking down.

"I got a tank if you're looking for something unusual," the Swede told me without skipping a beat, seemingly ignorant of the absurdity of the announcement. "Can take a few weeks, but I can get it over here to New York no problem. Talk to your friends Lou and Durrico in case they are interested," he said as if it all made sense. "Bazookas are a little tougher to get but if you give me a month I can get two."

"You can get a tank?" I asked him.

"A tank is not a problem. Parking it might be, but then again if you can afford a tank you can afford a place to put it."

Swede had the oddest accent. Sometimes he sounded Mexican and other times he sounded like he was from someplace like Romania.

"Okay, thanks," I said. I was never sure if the Swede was high on something potent or for real so I always played along.

He shook my hand and turned to join the conversation with Durrico, Lou and Lenny.

I turned away and that was when I saw Nancy. She was at the bar with another woman and a couple of men. I noticed her because she was looking at me. With Wack eyeing me I was too distracted to smile at her but I was looking to step away from the people I was with so I moved over to her and her friends. They were only a few yards away.

I quickly noticed they didn't have a bottle of Moët with them and with a glance I could see they were professionals, either lawyers or accountants. They wore suits with white shirts and colorful ties. Glancing back at my crowd, I could see they were all in black and only Durrico wore a tie.

"You look familiar," she said to me as I approached.

"I'm glad I do," I said, trying to sound cool. She, however, was above that. She had no pretension and it threw me off. Most women in the club were either defensive, since so many of the guys were assholes, or they were flirty, looking for free hits of coke.

Nancy was pretty but in a more subtle way than Rebecca. She was petite, with shoulder length brown hair and forgiving brown eyes. She was also wearing a brown outfit that looked like she had gone to Visage straight from work.

"Where do you think you know me from?" I asked.

"I was a substitute teacher at Molloy last year. You were in a meeting I was in. I think it was for the Catholic Teachers Association. You went out of your way to be nice to me, but I'm sorry, I can't remember your name," she told me.

"Daniel," I said, reaching my hand to her. She took it and smiled. "Nancy," she said.

I did remember her. "You said some smart things about having the kids read some of the poetry they were studying out loud. I remember agreeing with you and really liking the idea," I told her.

"I did say that," she replied, gesturing to the "boys" I was with, "So you're Daniel in the Lion's Den, huh?"

"Why do you say that?" I asked.

"Just the way you seem jittery."

She gave me a jolt. I didn't move. She laughed. "Kidding," she said. I knew she was right. "Do you want to meet my friends?" she asked. She leaned in. "I don't know these guys. They were here when we came in. The girl is my friend from school, Brenda."

"Not now," I told her. "Another time."

"Okay." She was uncomfortable and I could see it. "Are you still teaching?" she asked. "I only ask because I didn't see you at the last meeting the Association had."

I shook my head.

"Oh, you teaching in public school now?" she asked.

"I'm not teaching anymore. I'm writing a novel," I told her. It sounded stupid to me but she ate it up.

"Cool," she said. "I want to write a novel someday but teaching is exhausting."

"That's why I left," I said. I took another look at her. She was smart. I saw that in her eyes; she looked at you when she talked to you. She was pretty and certainly interested in looking good but nothing like Rebecca's obsession with being the only female in the room.

As Nancy and I had our conversation I noticed Rebecca's smiling and flirting with Durrico. Lou seemingly laughed along as they were all flying high on the coke, but I started noticing things like Rebecca allowing her hand to touch Durrico's as she moved to the bar to sip her champagne and how Durrico edged closer to her, all the while focusing his eyes on Lou to make sure Lou didn't see. But Lou saw it all and the sting of the champagne conversation was still fresh.

Everything was moving so quickly now that Lenny "The Roach" had appeared with the Swede and their ladies. It was a party with everyone looking hot and sexy with the music pulsating and the cocaine and champagne creating all the momentum. I was thinking who cared what champagne we drank and who cared who provided the coke. The only important thing was that there was a party going on and I wasn't paying for it.

"Wow, she's hot," Nancy said to me, shaking me out of my spell. She gestured to Rebecca and I smirked. "I mean, as a girl, I can even say, she's hot."

I smiled at her. She was sweet and funny. Her friend Brenda had hit it off with one of the attorneys, so she left Nancy. Nancy didn't have her car with her. "I should take a cab home."

"I'll take you home," I said to her. "But it's early. Stay a while."

Nancy looked at her watch. "It's ten already. I have a seven forty-five class in the morning."

"Wait," I said. I moved over to Lou and asked him for the vial. "I just want the girl to have a little hit," I said. Lou grinned and discreetly handed me the vial.

I walked back to Nancy. "Go into the ladies' room and do a hit."

"I never did coke," she told me, her big brown eyes looking

up at me. I walked over to Rebecca. "My friend wants to do a line and she's never done it before."

Rebecca nodded. "Don't worry, sweetie. I'll take care of her." Rebecca led a hesitant Nancy into the ladies' room.

That's when Durrico got up and left our table, as if he didn't want to make a big deal out of saying goodbye to Rebecca.

"I'm going to the Red Patriot to see a girl about my hard on," he said. We all knew he was seeing a Spanish hostess over there.

As soon as Durrico left Lou leaned in to me and said, "Fuck him."

"I still have to pay him."

"Yeah, you still do," Lou said. He leaned over and whispered in my ear. "I got the Contractor's Conference at the Waldorf this Saturday night. I need you."

"Okay," I said.

Lou nodded to Lenny. "I don't want that sleazebag sitting with us. Make sure he doesn't. Save the seat for your girl."

It was nice to hear Lou refer to Nancy as my girl. I moved over the seats giving Lenny a look, but careful not to start a nasty incident.

Lou stood up and discreetly handed Lenny "The Roach" a wad of cash. Several vials of cocaine quickly appeared from Lenny's jacket pocket and he passed them to Lou.

I learned from watching Lou that the best way to make a deal with the drugs was out in the open at the bar, since security guards never paid much attention.

Lou opened up to me. "Fucking Rebecca. Now she doesn't like Moët. She drank so much of it this week with me that she had to piss a gallon or two of it."

"She was just trying to impress people," I said.

Lou didn't respond verbally but he understood what I meant, and it was tough on him that I saw what he figured to be a major slight by Durrico.

As soon as Nancy and Rebecca came out of the ladies' room, Lou got us a table in one of Visage's most sought-after VIP rooms. It was the Blue Room, where everything glowed in a blue light and our table overlooked the entire swimming pool area. From that vantage point we could see the swimmers, male and female, eventually go nude.

Rebecca and Nancy sat next to each other talking a-mile-on-coke second, leaving me the only sober one at the table. Eventually Lou got into their conversation as well and I felt completely left out. So I asked for the vial, went into the men's room and, once in the stall, did a hit. I came out and looked into the mirror. Wack was standing behind me. He startled me and just stared. I thought he had left with Durrico. I tried to move past him but he got in my way. We were alone in the bathroom.

"The entire ten grand on Sunday or you will bleed," he said to me.

I edged past him without saying a word and felt my heart pounding *through* my chest. Getting threatened with a beating right after you did a hit of coke was not the best thing for the organ.

I went back to the table and sat next to Nancy. She took a look at me and said, "You okay?"

"I'm okay," I lied.

I felt her hand on my leg. "Nice," I said. Before I could say another word, she kissed me and I was kissing her back. I was aware of enough to glance at Lou and he had his mouth all over Rebecca's. The blue room was a great place to get high, make out and sometimes even get a hand job or get your hand up *her* thigh.

I could hear "Bad Girls" playing overhead as I allowed myself to fade into the sensuality of the moment. Nights at Visage were a blur.

Somewhere around two a.m. I drove Lou back to Rebecca's. He told me to take the car so I did. I drove Nancy back to my place. Lou left me with what was left in the vial of coke so Nancy and I did it as I drove through the Midtown Tunnel, across the Long Island Expressway and to my apartment.

I parked the car and Nancy and I were kissing. I found the keys to my building as mostly working-class people were walking to the bus stop to go to work.

"We have to see the sun come up," I told Nancy. We stood on my roof facing east and there it was, rising majestically up over the Whitestone Bridge, slowly shoving the night back to where it had come from: the other side of the world.

With the light facing us when we turned around we could see the city skyline.

I took Nancy back to my apartment, leaving the curtains down. "I have to be at work in three hours," she said. I turned on my radio. "Bad Girls" was playing again. I walked up to Nancy (who hadn't moved) and slid her dress up over her hips. I pulled down her stockings and her panties.

I gently put her down on the bed. I kissed her mouth feeling her hands rummaging for my penis. She opened my zipper, grabbed my cock and sucked on it. I put my face down in her crotch. We were a crumbled mess of limbs and torsos in our awkward attempt at sixty-nine when I decided to put both my arms under her bottom, turn her to face me and enter her.

We fucked crazily for what seemed like hours but in reality was probably only minutes. We locked lips driven by drugs, booze and lust. I felt her growing wet and though I was hard I knew I couldn't come because of the coke. So when I felt her slow down, I pulled out and let her suck me some more. She did and in the tiny rays of light coming through my curtains falling across her face I could see how pretty she really was. Her features were feminine and soft and when she looked at me with those big brown eyes I came. She wiggled underneath me pulling my cock deeper into her mouth.

All the life drained out of me. I fell over her and closed my eyes. I felt her breathing underneath me. I could see the gentle outline of her profile as I fell asleep.

4

I WAS STILL IN THE SAME position when Nancy moved. She looked at her watch. "Oh, my God," she said, as she pushed me aside and struggled to get up. "It's noon," she told me. "Where's your phone?" I nodded to the phone across the room and vaguely remember watching her until I fell back into a deep sleep.

It was dark out when I woke up. I needed water so I went to the sink and drank right from the faucet. I ripped all my clothes off, threw them in a corner and took a shower.

I checked my calendar on the wall and the day was circled. There was a game I wanted to get in. I had nothing to eat in the refrigerator so I drove to my friend Michael's restaurant seeing the rush-hour traffic heading out of the city where everyone who worked a full day was now going home. Michael had an Italian restaurant on Woodhaven Boulevard. I walked in; he saw me and waved me over to a table in the back near the bar.

"Do That to Me One More Time" was playing on the stereo just loud enough for me to hear the lyrics.

I knew there was the weekly game at the social club across the street on the corner. It was high rollers and they were all mobbed-up guys and sometimes the atmosphere got a little wild but there was money to be made. It was a monthly game run by a guy named Gabe, a bookie with big-time friends, and that was the game I wanted to be in.

"Wild night, huh?" Michael asked as soon as I sat down.

"Yeah, they are all that way now," I said getting comfortable in the dim light. Michael was a long-time friend from the neighborhood and he quickly told the waiter to bring me a plate of veal Parmesan, some salad, and a scotch and soda.

Michael was married to his high school girlfriend, Lillian, and they had two kids. He was slim, always liked wearing a dark suit and tie, and had his deep black hair combed back. He had an olive complexion with watery light brown eyes. He worked with his father in the restaurant. Both men worked twelve hour days with one day off a week and it was his father's day off.

"I look around and it's so weird now," he said.

"You being philosophical?" I asked.

Michael sipped his own drink as he eyed the waiters and the orders and empty plates they brought to and from the kitchen. "Yeah, I am."

"About?"

"I get this feeing, Danny. What I mean is this: I look around to see who comes into my place, right? Sure, I got the regulars who never seem to change but the other day my wife was sitting here and I remember her being a flower child when I met her, right? Right out of high school she was an idealist," he said. "We were all idealists back then."

"Yeah, you can say that. You had that band of yours," I said.

"Exactly. I loved folk singing and playing guitar. I loved writing my tunes. I wanted to change the world but then the seventies come along and what? The hippies die off and we got rock and roll and drugs. Okay, I could dig that. But we still had the poetry. That didn't go away. But tell me, Danny, what do we have *now*?" he asked.

I looked at him and he had this sincere flush to his face. "I don't have an answer," I said.

"Neither do I but I don't like it. The *Godfather* movie changed it all. I got more wannabes walking into my joint than ever before. They all want to act like they run something and they all act tough," Michael said.

"Lou and Durrico are real and they didn't need some movie to tell them who they were," I said.

"Lou and Durrico are real for sure. I remember back in high school when Lou was a freshman selling pot to seniors. He also was into Dylan before anybody heard of Dylan around here," Michael said. "Durrico was pushing people around when he was in his diapers, giving orders in kindergarten, but that's not what I mean."

"Okay," I said.

"I come up with what I feel and I'll let you know. It's like thunder. I hear it out there but I don't have a name for it yet."

"Tell me about the game," I said as I sipped my scotch.

Michael put down his drink. "I saw Gabe earlier. He stopped by for lunch. You need two grand just to sit at the table tonight."

I nodded. I had two grand in my wallet.

"Most of the guys playing are all wannabes and some B-list wannabe boys. No money there. The big player is a guy named Lloyd," he said.

"Lloyd?" I asked.

"A Jew from Bayside. Makes good money with his used car business in Whitestone. He's the sucker at the table. Only thing is—he *is* good. The other thing is—don't fuck with him. Gabe gets good deals on cars over there with him and he doesn't want to fuck that up," Michael said. "They all come in here to eat and they like my menu."

I listened closely because I knew the only way I could get into that game was by Michael vouching for me. He was a straight shooter and though he knew a lot of wise guys he wasn't one of them. He had the ability to feed them, have conversations with them, but stay clear of them. It was as if they liked him enough to eat in his place and not get him in trouble with the law.

I saw the paper on Michael's table and the front page was all about the transit strike already on day four. I couldn't care less. Like everybody else, I knew that nobody in their right mind took a bus or a train if they wanted to get to their destination within a year.

I ate my veal when it came and washed it down with another scotch. I hung out with Michael, telling him about my situation with Durrico, Lou and his new obsession, Rebecca, and my one-night stand with Nancy. In fact, before I had come to Michael's I found that Nancy left me her number but I was too focused on the game ahead to call her. The game didn't start until ten and I knew there was a pay phone on the corner but I waited knowing that she might be sleeping off the crazy night before and I didn't want to wake her.

When it came time, I left a few bucks for my dinner, shook hands with Michael and went across the street. A guy in his fifties, medium build with thick dark gray hair let me in. He was wearing a leather jacket. "Michael said it was okay for me. I'm Danny Ferraro," I said.

"I don't need your last name," he said nodding as if I was on a list in his head and gestured for me to go down stairs.

The game was held in the basement with a small bar in the back. I got a scotch from a pretty chestnut-haired girl at the bar and went up to Gabe, who I already knew, and thanked him for letting me in the game. He was a bulky guy, shorter than me but with huge shoulders. I looked at the table. "Anywhere?"

He nodded so I sat next to the dealer, a young guy in a red vest and white shirt. *Style*, I said to myself. I half-smiled to anyone who looked at me and waited for the game to start.

We played five-card stud and after going through two rounds I knew how everyone played at the table. I knew I was the best player and the high roller, Lloyd, was itching to get into a big hand and get lucky.

Somewhere around midnight a big guy in his thirties in a loose black shirt with a husky voice excused himself from the game and gave the waitress a hundred-dollar bill asking if he could do a line of coke off her nipple.

I hadn't been paying attention to him since his play was poor but he had deep-set eyes and kept watching the chips slide back and forth across the table but never to his stack.

Clearly the waitress, with dimples and large earrings, had done it before because she snatched the bill out his hand, pulled down her halter-top and leaned back on the bar.

From where I was sitting I could hardly see her breasts but I could see him sprinkle white powder on both nipples.

"You said one nipple," she told him.

"I lied," he answered.

He snorted the line and licked her nipple.

"No licking," the waitress told him.

"How about some fucking?" he asked.

"Play poker or leave," Gabe growled.

The husky-voiced guy lowered his head like a dog that had just been reprimanded by its owner and sat down at the table but he only played a few more hands before he left.

By two in the morning I was up a grand. By three I was up another.

Gabe paid the pretty waitress who waited outside for a cab to take her home.

"What a pair of tits," someone said.

"Play poker. She's my cousin's kid," Gabe told the table.

It was four in the morning when I got the position I wanted with the cards I wanted up against Lloyd. I wanted to bet first. My hole cards were an ace and a ten and I was dealt an ace showing. So I had a pair of aces. Lloyd had a king showing. I watched him. He seemed calm but I knew he was pretending to be relaxed. He had a "tell" that gave away his hand and he gave away that it was big. His "tell" was this: all through the night he would look into the eyes of the player he was playing but he never looked into their eyes when he had a big hand. So, this time he was looking away from me.

I bet big and watched him. He called quickly, never looking *at* me.

Everyone else went out. Gabe went out and watched me. My next card was a five of clubs and Lloyd drew a three of

hearts. I bet big and again he quickly called. He saw my ace
so he must have figured me for a pair. So, in order for him
to stay "in" and keep calling he had to have trip kings or
else he thought I was bluffing. He was setting me up for a
big takedown.

By the time we got to our last card, dealt face down, the
pot was up to nearly five grand. I knew I should go out. I only
had the pair of aces and Lloyd was sticking to me like glue. I
didn't think he was on a draw so he must have had the trip
kings and he was playing it cagey. I figured I'd buy one more
card. I was a little ahead for the night so if I didn't catch anything on the last card, I'd go out when he bet. But I caught
another ace dealt face down and now I had trip aces and I
had Lloyd dead in the water.

I checked. Lloyd raised. I felt my heart beat. I did all I
could to relax and pretend I didn't have the "nuts." I had
him dead to rights. Even if he had the three kings I put him
on, I had him.

I took a moment. I felt Gabe drilling through me with his
stare. I knew Lloyd wanted me to check raise. I knew I should
have just called so I didn't look like a pig but I needed the
money. I glanced at the cash Lloyd had in front of him. I
knew I had two grand left to bet. I knew that if I raised, Lloyd
had to call. It was a bad beat he could never see coming, so
despite the hell I knew I was going to get, I went for it.

"I raise," I said. I threw in my last remaining cash.

I looked up at Lloyd. He had a thin face, a full head of
gray hair and small blue eyes. I saw him hesitate. He knew
something wasn't right but there was one element of the
game that no one could figure on and that was *luck*. He had
made all the right moves, he drew me into his trap, but with

the last card I caught lightning as if it was a bolt from the sky and now I wanted a big payoff.

He knew that I knew he had no choice but to call me. No one can lay down three kings in a spot like that. He reached down, pushed his two grand into the pot and looked at me. I hated to turn over my cards. I showed the trip aces with reluctance.

Lloyd threw himself back in his chair. "Lucky fuck," he said. He looked at Gabe who cringed. Gabe didn't even look at me but looked at one of his guys in the corner.

I dragged in the chips. "I was lucky. Did you have kings?" I asked.

Lloyd threw over his trip kings. "Lucky fuck," someone else said, directed at me.

We played a few more hands, which I was sure to lose, hoping Gabe would let me off the hook. I played against Lloyd and made sure he won some small pots from me, and a couple of hands I even threw away the winning hand to make sure he won. Around five in the morning the game broke up. Everyone said goodbye to everyone else but no one said a word to me.

I went outside. I could see people standing at the bus stop across the street getting ready to go to work. I walked to my car and opened my door and just as I did one of Gabe's guys came up behind me and punched me in the side of the face, my blind side, and knocked me into my car.

I woke up a few minutes later behind the wheel with a pain shooting through my jaw. I knew it wasn't broken but it hurt like hell. I drove home and checked my wallet. The cash was still all there. I had over six grand or more and a pain under my right ear as payback from Gabe for taking

down his moneybags but it was worth it, I thought to myself.
I tripled my bankroll.

I went home and popped a few Seconals and felt better as
the pain faded. I could relax a little now that I had some real
cash to pay off Durrico.

5

I LAY LOW THE NEXT FEW days doing some odd pickups for Lou and somewhere in there I called Nancy and asked her out to dinner. I had a few bucks to spend so I took her out to Michael's where we had a bottle of wine and some delicious pasta.

"Crazy Little Thing Called Love" was playing in the background. "I hate that fucking song," I told her.

"How come?"

"Just hate it. Don't you sometimes either hate or love a thing and you don't know why?"

Nancy shot me a sweet smile and continued with her meal.

When Michael sat with us I could see by the way he looked at her that he enjoyed Nancy's intelligence and soft features and easy-going manner.

"My father started this place as a pizza parlor twenty-five years ago. After my mother died I came in and changed the menu a little with my own veal dish and a few special pastas but it's basically the same old place my father created," he told her.

"My grandmother loved to cook Italian. She was from Bari," Nancy told him.

I could see she enjoyed talking about Italian–American food and the family history of the restaurant. And later, during our dessert of Italian cookies, I saw that she was uniquely inquisitive, sharing with me that she wanted to pursue her education and get a master's degree in sociology.

After Michael left our table I shared with Nancy the conversation I had had with Michael about the sixties and seventies being something in the distant past and now we were entering a new decade and something new was in the air. I half believed it but I knew Michael did.

Nancy looked at Michael as he directed his waiters. "He's insightful," she said.

"Does he make sense?"

"I think so. I feel something in the air. It makes me think of John Lennon," she said.

"What does?"

"Your friend, I think. Something about him. Sensitive," she answered. "I love Lennon and Ono. Who do you listen to?"

I gave her the answer I thought she wanted to hear. I loved all the "regulars" I told her. I was enjoying watching her. I smiled and she saw me smile at her.

"I love to hear about people and what makes them do the things they do," she told me. She had a sparkle that came from her intellect. We spoke about her growing up in Mineola and how her father worked for the county planner's office and how her mother was a schoolteacher and how she was an only child. She told me she was close to her parents and how she would never want to let them down.

"They probably have your future husband picked out already," I said to her.

"They do. His name is Brian. He's a lawyer from Garden City. We date once in a while. He has a bit of an ego so I think he wants me to beg for him to propose or something," she said with a tiny smile.

The light in the restaurant was purposely dim and I was glad since I was sure she didn't see me cringe a little when she mentioned this lawyer she was dating who was clearly interested in her. "Do you like him?" I had to ask.

"I do," she said.

"Then why are you here?" I said trying not to sound spiteful but truly inquisitive. "Because he didn't ask you out tonight?"

"No, I'm here because I like you, too, Danny," she said.

It wasn't what she said that touched me but how she said it. She put down her fork and got quiet. "I was really embarrassed about the other night. I never did that before," she told me.

"Coming back to my place?" I asked.

"Yes. But not just that. All that we did. We just met and we had sex. It's not something I do, Danny. I also missed my class without calling in. I was humiliated by what I did with you and with school. If you didn't call me I would have felt like such a fool."

"I like you, Nancy."

"Do you? But why did we do all that stuff? I mean, I'm not an innocent kid but to go home and make love like that and we don't know one another at all," she said. I could see she was getting upset.

"We didn't respect the situation is what you're saying?"

"Yes. I mean, I went to your house of my own free will. I wanted to be 'with you' sometime, but not the first time, yet it happened so fast." She looked down. She was being honest and typical me I figured I was lucky that I had met a girl who liked sex and drugs and rock and roll.

"It was the coke, Nancy," I told her.

She looked up, her dark eyes burning brightly. "It was, right?"

"It was," I said feeling I should tell her that I was sorry so I did.

"You don't have to be," she said quickly. "But I can't do it again, Danny."

I nodded but I was disappointed. I liked her body. I still remembered how giving she was. I didn't have a girlfriend. I was alone and clearly didn't feel it much until that moment.

"Can we be friends?" she asked.

That was something I didn't want to hear. I felt rejected. Now it was my time to look away.

She saw I was hurt. "You liked me that much?"

"I said it," I told her.

"But is that how to act with a girl you like?"

I watched her closely. She was even more delicate-looking than ever.

"I want to get married eventually, Danny. Your lifestyle doesn't point to you being the settling-down kind of guy. You quit your job. How do you live? What do you live on?"

"I gamble," I told her. "Cards mainly."

"Really? What about your novel?" she asked sincerely.

"I need to get back to it. I want to write. I can't work for someone. I hate it. I hate having 'hours.' I hate having to answer to someone. Your lawyer guy sounds right for you," I said sharply.

Nancy reached across the table and took my hand. "Don't say it that *that* way, please."

"What way?"

"That Brian is my type because he is everything you are not. He's not adventurous, he's not talented and he's not exciting."

I half smiled. "I'm all that?" I asked.

"Yes, and sexy," she said. "That's why I am here. Though you are dangerous and that worries me.

After dinner we took my car and drove to Maurice Park and walked to one of the benches. The park keeper's shack had been burned down years earlier and the city never replaced or fixed up the rotting wood that remained. We sat in silence listening to the cars pass east and west on the Long Island Expressway.

It was chilly out but we both had on our jackets and it seemed to be warm enough sitting outside with them on. I liked the chilly night air and more than that I liked sitting outside in it talking and just stargazing and dreaming.

"My grandfather was a hero and look how his grandson is turning out," I said. I felt stupid saying what I just did, since my tone was filled with self-pity.

Nancy kept quiet. "You told me a little that night. How he killed that Nazi on the Brooklyn Docks. How he worked hard all his life to make a life for your mother. How gangsters nearly killed him," she said remembering a lot of our conversation from the night at Visage.

"I wrote the first three chapters. I open the novel on the dock. It's two in the morning on a chilly night like this and my grandfather sees this spy laying explosives on the boat. He comes up from behind him and never saw that the Nazi sympathizer had an ax pick in his hand. They fought for a half an hour nearly. My grandfather was hit several times and had to get stitches but he eventually killed the guy with the ax. He was my age when that happened," I told her.

"Who did he kill?"

"A German from the other side. A Nazi who was actually left here by submarine," I said remembering the story.

"You'll be a great writer," she said and took my hand.

"Why do you say that?"

"Just the way you just told the story. Maybe you're a natural-born storyteller," she said.

"What about you?" I asked.

She nestled in my arms. "I love teaching. They say high school kids are tough but they aren't really. They just want attention. Most of them are worried about how their lives will turn out." She looked up past me into the night sky. "One day I'd like to get my masters and teach in a college. I'd even travel and move to do that. I just need to build my resume and eventually save up the money for graduate school. But that's my dream."

"Did you ever read *Loon Lake?*"

"Doctorow's novel? Yes, I liked it."

"It's inspiring my novel."

"How?"

"It's the story of this guy in the Depression who has nothing but sees this beautiful naked blond woman in the window of a passing train in the middle of the night and by the end of the novel she's his lover and he becomes rich beyond imagination," I told her.

"Yes, I remember that now. It's dark and cynical though."

"What isn't?" I asked.

"He was poking fun at the American dream," she said.

"Yes, I know."

I leaned in and kissed her. I didn't hesitate and she didn't push me away either. The kiss was the most sensual I could remember having without drugs to enhance the sensation. While feeling her lips on mine I also felt the sensuality of the evening air, the far-away sounds, the cars zooming along the expressway making a sound like ocean waves at night.

I buried my face in her neck, breathing her in, closing my eyes, allowing her hair to fall across her face. I kissed her behind her ear and I felt her hand on my face gently pushing me back. "No, please," she said.

I leaned back. We shared a long look, eye to eye through the shadows and the half-light thrown down across from the lamp.

"I want to see you tomorrow," I told her despite knowing I had to work for Lou.

"I can't. I have a date with Brian," she said.

"We can meet after he drops you off," I said.

I could see a twinkle, just a tiny one, explode in her eyes. She was titillated by the notion of seeing one boy, then running out and seeing another. It was the same "tell" I looked for in poker players, that "something" that gave away who they were without a word. Nancy liked the kick, the rush, the excitement, though she was afraid of it. She was afraid because she might not be able to control it.

"I want to make love to you again, Nancy," I said.

"No, Danny. We're friends," she said.

"You are so sexy," I told her, putting my hand on her thigh. She shivered, wiggled on the bench and pushed me away. She stood. I stood and faced her. We were inches apart. She leaned in and kissed me tongue to tongue, driving her body into mine, grinding her groin into mine, and pushed me away again. She was breathing hard, shaking her head. "Please, take me to my car or I'll just walk back."

When I dropped her off she opened the door quickly, knowing that if she hesitated she wouldn't get out. "I can't be near you," she told me. "Please don't call."

"Don't call you? Why?"

I watched her get into her car without answering me and drive off. I sat parked in the middle of the street for a long time. I had found a woman I liked and realized I was as dangerous to her as I was to myself.

When I got home I sat behind my typewriter and wrote a few more pages of my novel. Yes, it was true that my grandfather had killed a Nazi sympathizer during World War II and yes, he was a hero. What I didn't tell Nancy was the rest of the story. My grandfather was a gambler who lived alone in a small apartment in Williamsburg, Brooklyn. He had also nearly killed another man, an acquaintance, with his fists when the man cursed in front of a woman. It happened on the corner of Richardson and Lorimer streets near McCarren Park in the 1950s. The man went into a coma but lived and my grandfather ran away and lived on the road for a few years. While he was away living on gambling, my grandmother left him and eventually my mother did, too.

My grandfather was a tough, self-contained man who drove away everyone because he couldn't control his dark side and his own inherent weaknesses.

But I wasn't going to write about that grandfather; I was going to write about the one who was a hero, the one I idolized and the one I wanted to be.

6

I SHOWED UP AT THE WALDORF Astoria Hotel on Saturday at seven p.m. dressed in my only suit and met Lou's personal banker Bruno Nardi in the front lobby. We went to the garage and took several heavy suitcases from his trunk filled with assorted bottles of alcohol and brought them up to Lou's suite, 1212.

We collected many buckets of ice from the ice machine down the hallway and filled the suite's bathtub. Bruno had also brought along several dozen plastic cups so in short time we had a homemade bar all set up. This saved Lou a fortune in ordering drinks from room service. Our makeshift bar had the basic fundamental food chain of booze including scotch, vodka, gin, whiskey and bourbon along with assorted sodas for mixed drinks. By the time Lou showed up in his tuxedo, Bruno and I were ready to meet the ladies and the contractors.

As soon as Lou entered the suite he turned to me. "Collect the ashtrays," he said.

I went around the suite picking up the hotel ashtrays and

placed all eight of them on the desk Lou was now using as his command central.

I watched as Lou pulled out several bags of cocaine and filled each tray with coke. When he was done he turned to me again.

"Okay, now put them back where you found them," he said. So I did.

In our short time together Bruno explained the evening to me so Lou didn't have to waste time telling me. It seemed that every April, the East Coast Contractors Conference had their annual dinner at the Waldorf. It was the time and place all the contractors would sit down together, share war stories and make deals.

Lou had already rented himself a suite a month in advance, along with four single rooms. There were going to be over three thousand contractors in the hotel having a big dinner, and while that was happening, Lou wanted me and Bruno to set up the suite and run everything while he was downstairs.

Lou's plan was simple. He hired six escorts. They would hang out in the suite, drink and eat, and after the dinner, Lou would invite those contractors he planned to do business with up to the suite. The contractors would mingle, have drinks, discuss business and they would check the girls out and pick the one they liked. At which time Lou put each of the call girls in a separate room.

I had learned from Lou that a lot of business was done over dinner, booze, cocaine and blowjobs. I had no idea where these businessmen found these ladies but they were in ample supply and ready to trade sex for money if the money was good.

Bruno explained to me that the banking business was a lot different but he was happy to be working for Lou. Bruno was a little older than me and married and I could tell how excited he was in anticipation of being around and interacting with professional call girls. As soon as they showed up he was tripping over himself getting the ladies drinks, asking them if they were at ease as they tried to relax in the suite.

My job, Bruno told me, was to make sure the girls were safe from the contractors and nobody was making any side deals with the businessmen for more sex and for that matter, any hotel guests who might just happen across the scene as well, as it had been known to happen in earlier years.

Though Bruno had already paid off hotel security, we still didn't want any problems with them by getting complaints from other hotel guests.

Also Lou didn't care if they did some side work while in the hotel, Bruno explained, but if they were going to make extra money he didn't want it done on his time when he was already paying them. I wasn't sure how much each lady was paid but I was thinking it was a couple of hundred in cash for each contractor she had sex with.

Lou paid for the sex for those contractors he wanted to do business with and in return he expected them to make it easy for his trucks to dump their loads at their sites without worrying about state or federal regulations, including permit applications and payoffs to the guys who ran the dumps and of course the high fees that came along with them.

Lou explained to me that it was cheaper for him to send his trucks to, say, North Carolina to dump medical waste than to pay the exuberant dumping fees on Staten Island.

Some of the most sought-after businessmen for Lou were those contractors who had access to dumping grounds with low fees. New York and New Jersey had tough dumping site regulations but some states had lax regulations on what could be dumped and how much. Lou learned that with a few bribes like what he was doing in the suite, the regulators, paid off by the contracts, would look the other way.

"The ladies can have a few drinks but don't let them get drunk," Bruno said to me nervously several times.

Weeks ago, Lou had told me that Bruno was now his private banker and he had his former bank loan Lou two million in cash to his business. "Bruno gets first pick of girls once we start. But he won't do a thing, I know it. He's loyal to the wife so I doubt he'll get laid," Lou joked when he arrived in the suite.

Bruno also shared with me earlier that Lou found the girls through several friends who knew some of them either personally or professionally. They were all very different and their levels of experience all varied.

I had a couple of scotch and sodas when Lou asked me to sit next to him at his desk and poured out a long line of coke in front of us. He handed me a clean straw. "Partake, pal," he said generously.

I placed the straw in my right nostril and inhaled a little of the line. I felt a blast of heated energy race into my head through my sinuses.

I sat back and handed the straw to Lou but he declined it and pulled out his own straw and did a line.

That's when I heard Bruno call to us from the door. "The ladies are here," he told us.

I stood up as the girls came in all at once. One by one they entered the suite. I immediately noticed that one of them was actually in charge. Susie was a little older than the others and spoke for them all. In her early thirties, she was wearing nothing but black lingerie. She stepped into the suite with a coat over her shoulders but she quickly handed it to Bruno, revealing the lingerie.

Joy was a very quiet bleached blond from Orlando in a bright blue cocktail dress and white high heels. Dotty was a single mother who told me later on that it was the first time she was ever having sex for money and she was scared, but she couldn't pay the taxes on her small house in Patchogue so when the offer came to "entertain" at the Waldorf she took it. Lena was a soft-spoken dancer with a trim tanned body wearing a tight-fitting black dress. Elle was Italian and Russian and she seemed to be the most outgoing. She was tall with wild black hair and loved to curse and joke around.

"Hello ladies," Lou said to them with his most charming grin. "I put out a few lines for you. Enjoy but don't overdo it. There's a long night of work ahead of us," Lou told them.

One by one the girls walked over to the desk, picked up a straw Lou left for them and did a line.

Bruno and I watched them and all the while I noticed how Susie made a point of not only watching how much coke each lady snorted but she also stayed away from the desk herself.

Lou handed her a drink, clearly knowing what she liked, and the two of them discreetly moved away from everyone else and spoke in whispers to one another.

I could see that the girls were anxious so I flirted with all of them, starting with small talk and then enthusiastically talking about my favorite topic—poker—and of course my own novel. Though seemingly interested they all paid extra attention when I told them how, when I used to teach high school English, I got my students into it by throwing in poker references.

"I would tell them that Hemingway's stuff was like a trip aces. Tough to get and hard to enjoy," I said. "Fitzgerald is like a straight flush. Pretty to look at and in the end potent."

The girls chimed in that they knew the authors' names from high school and gave me big smiles. I was sure none of them had read any of the novelists I mentioned but we had fun killing time.

I whetted their interest—lying that I was already talking to publishers about my novel. Lena was the most educated and we had a short discussion about Sylvia Plath, who she adored, and we both were soon plastered on scotch and soda as we hung out in the suite. "I love her poems about death," she said.

I was about to ask her to elaborate when Lou reappeared and waved me over. "How's it going?"

"Good. I'm keeping them entertained," I said.

"I hear. You're talking about books," he smirked. "Like what, any of them read?"

I could sense he was on edge so I didn't respond.

"I keep calling Rebecca. It bugs me she isn't by her phone," he said checking his watch.

"It's early," I said.

"Could be," he answered. "Downstairs they are probably having dessert right now."

Lou went back to his desk, checking out a list of contractors' names he had written down.

Just then Lena, holding a glass, walked over to me and whispered that she wanted to take me to one of the rooms.

"Another night," I told her, finding her hard to resist. "I have to keep my eye on things."

Lena was adorable and only twenty-three and I was really

drunk. We talked about the theater and her career, which seemed to have more to do with her passion for dancing than any real income, and that led her to having sex for money.

"Not to bring it up but how do you have sex with some of these contractor guys? I mean, well, you know what I mean."

"I get drunk."

"And that works?"

"Most men are very sweet," she said.

"But some of these guys are going to be fat and in their fifties," I said.

"It really bothers you?" she asked. The other girls were talking among themselves and picking on the food tray Lou had room service brought in for them.

"Kind of, yeah. I mean, you're really nice and pretty and everything and I hate to see you with those guys. I mean, I know I couldn't have sex with a woman I didn't think was at least attractive," I told her.

"Don't judge me," she said.

"I didn't mean to," I replied.

"I'll make some good money tonight. Cash. I need rent, I need clothes and I need food. I also have to pay for my studio where I teach kids how to dance and I am not making my monthly nut yet. Prices for everything are going up. Plus, I like sex," she grinned.

She jumped up and started to dance around the room. It looked as if she was doing modern dance movements. She was nimble and supple and so slim I was amazed how aesthetic it all was, watching her slim body flow through the shadows in the dimly lit room.

"You are really good," I told her.

"I came here two years ago from Cleveland right out of my junior year of college. I didn't want to put off living my dream anymore," she told me, hardly out of breath as she danced around the room.

Even the other girls were watching her in awe.

"You're good," Joy said. "When you said you were a dancer I thought you meant stripper."

"I do that too sometimes," Lena said, not once losing her rhythm.

"This is living your dream?" I whispered leaning into her, hoping not to sound sarcastic.

"Yes! We are in the Waldorf in New York City with ashtrays filled with cocaine and I am *not* in Cleveland tonight, am I?"

Lena looked delicate but she really wasn't. She was as hard as any sidewalk in New York City with an exterior built to defy rejection and humiliation with idealism, youthful arrogance and simple ignorance as her defense.

I was enjoying watching her dance so much I didn't want to stop her. I took notice of her tiny breasts, tiny feet and finely muscled legs as she swirled around the hotel room, making each movement irresistible.

Lou shouted to me, taking me out of my trance. "The boys are here."

I looked at the girls but they had also heard Lou. They took out their face mirrors and checked their makeup.

Lena stopped moving and smiled at me. "Maybe you and me later," she smiled. All at once the girls moved toward the contractors as Lou smiled and shook hands, gesturing to Susie who introduced the ladies.

Lou was sitting at a big table, suddenly surrounded by over

a dozen guys in tuxedos smoking cigars and sipping drinks. The guys were all ages, shapes and sizes and were either rugged with sundrenched faces from being outdoors, or heavyset bosses who did their work indoors behind a desk like Lou did his.

The girls quickly started mingling, sipping cocktails and flirting as they were waiting to be chosen. They got paid for each guy they took back to a room so they wanted to get picked.

The smartest in the room was Susie, who even made me hot right after my encounter with Lena. Susie was nearly nude in her black lingerie and heels and most of the men were vying for her attention, making me realize that they had it backwards—she was really choosing them. She was there for the money—not the ego gratification, and certainly not for them. With her round, midwestern face, large light blue eyes and blond hair cut as if someone put a bowl on her head, she wasn't the typical-looking call girl but she was the center of attention in that suite and the smartest person in the room.

* * *

THE NIGHT TOOK ON THE CHAOTIC rumblings that usually go along with drinking scotch and doing lines. I had nothing in common with anyone at the party so I stood back, aloof and detached with my hands folded in front of me and with my mind racing like a stampede of runaway horses.

I checked myself out in the mirror, eyeing my dark blue tie, light blue shirt and dark blue sports jacket, the clothes I wore when teaching those high school classes, realizing I probably looked like a bodyguard who was carrying.

The need for a gun never occurred to me since I figured Lou to be the scariest one in the room, but then again one of these contractors could be some "big deal" also and I would have no idea.

Not wanting to think too much I took in the opulence of the room, the mahogany desk, the combination of dark green painted walls and wood molding and the elegant, at least to me, rug in the middle of the floor and pondered how the men in the room were wealthy only because they knew how to bury garbage, knock down structures or lay cement.

The more I thought about this the more I thought about Nancy, but I knew calling her in the state I was in was not a good idea.

I also needed to be on my toes since my job was to escort each girl and each contractor to their private room, hand them the key and head back to the suite. I grew more and more restless as the night wore on.

However, at one point Lou waved me over from my place in the corner.

"This guy George has been in his room with that Joy broad too long. If they didn't elope I have no idea what they're doing. Check them out," Lou said.

He handed me a key and I left the suite. Lou had rented three rooms on the twelfth floor and two more on the tenth. Most of the girls liked a couple of minutes in the room by themselves as they waited for their next "john." The guys needed a few drinks and a couple of lines to get the courage to pick and choose. They all had fantasies. I learned this by talking with the girls on our walks and elevator trips.

Some of the guys picked the girl they did probably because they looked like their secretaries or younger versions of their wives and some even divulged that they chose their particular girl because she looked like their daughter.

All the girls except Susie flirted with me, figuring I knew Lou well so I must be someone important or I was his bodyguard, and that turned them on.

George and Joy were on the same floor as the suite. When I reached the door I knocked. Nothing. I knocked again but I didn't want to make too much noise so I opened the locked door and entered the room.

When I did I immediately saw this heavyset contractor on his back on the bed, naked, with his legs up in the air. Joy was standing at his crotch with a finger wrapped in a condom up his ass while she was jerking him off.

She looked at me and smirked. "Sorry it's taking so long but he did too much blow and now he can't come," she said.

Not very happy with the visual image now in my brain, I quickly turned around, closed the door and headed back to the suite and explained to Lou what I saw.

"Fuckin' knuckleheads. George is my wife's uncle. What can I do?"

* * *

I HARDLY SAW LENA DURING THE swirl of activity and when I did she was coked out. One of the guys she saw, a young boss from North Carolina, got her so high from his coke batch she moved around like in a speed trance.

Some moments I'd be in the suite and there'd be no girls left since all were working in the other rooms. I sat with Lou listening to him rile Bruno, edging him to take one of the girls.

"Which one you like, Bruno?" he asked.

Bruno would demur, trying to change the subject by bringing up the contractors who Lou needed to follow up on the following week. Lou had a great mind for numbers and names I found out that night. He lived on favors and transactions, knowing which contractor needed what kind of equipment and how much he'd pay for it.

When Susie came back from one trip, Bruno nodded to Lou that he wanted Susie. Lou applauded and the entire room cheered. Bruno turned red as Susie took his hand and led him out of the suite. I got the key to one of the rooms and led Bruno and Susie to theirs.

I noticed in all my trips that when the couples left their rooms, the ladies all took the arms of the men they had been with. I wasn't sure if it was just something to do to keep hotel security off their backs by making them look like a "real" couple or if it was truly a sincere sign of affection. The ladies were smiling when they left the rooms and the men looked satisfied. I figured these particular guys could afford big tips so the ladies were happy since they were getting paid twice and the guys were happy that Lou was paying their initial fee for some great sex. Everyone seemed to like a free ride though in all reality none of it was free.

On her last trip Susie grabbed my arm and whispered, "You don't like me?"

I was taken aback. She took me by the arm and led me out of the suite to a room. Once alone in the room with Susie I sat back in a big comfortable chair and Susie handed me a hundred bucks. "Here."

"What's this for?"

"My way of thanking you for looking after the girls. They're mine and Lou's responsibility and I think you are doing a good job," she said.

I pocketed the cash but was really surprised.

"Some jerks would be hassling my girls and you're not, so you're not a jerk. Let me suck your cock while we're here. I think you're cute," she told me.

Well, I have to say that seeing her ass hanging out all night in the suite got me excited but before she could unzip my pants I put my hand gently on her arm. "I have to tell you something. I got a girl on my mind. I like her a lot so I don't think I can do this. Though I have to say you are tempting," I said.

Susie backed off. "You're different. Lou said you're a writer?" she asked as she went to the bathroom to clean up, wash her hands and apply more makeup.

"Yeah," I answered not wanting to elaborate.

Once in the hallway she took my arm as we walked back to the suite. "Do you tell all the girls to take walks like this back to the suite?"

"I do," she answered. "Makes for a nice and happy couple."

* * *

THE SEX AND DRINKING WENT ON until around three a.m., as the contractors eventually made their way home to their families or their own hotel rooms. Toward the end of the night the only people in the suite were Lou, Bruno, me, and all the girls.

Everything was winding down when Bruno, hunched over the table doing lines of coke, lost it.

"I'm hot, man," he said. He undid his shirt, pulled it off and sat down at the table bare-chested.

"You got man boobs," Lou said matter-of-factly and Bruno reacted by sitting back with a sheepish grin. He stood up and pulled down his pants and underwear.

"Suck my cock somebody," he shouted.

Lou glared at him. "Cool it," he said sharply.

"I couldn't come before, Lou," Bruno whined a little like complaining to his father.

"You were too coked up," Susie told him to his face, not interested in taking the blame for his inadequacies.

Bruno was now totally naked. He did the last line of blow on the table and started doing some kind of manic dance in front of us all, rubbing the remnants of coke on his cock forcing me and Lou to exchange looks of disgust.

"I hear that keeps you hard," Bruno told us.

Lou looked like he wanted to yell at him but after assessing the complete absurdity he chuckled instead.

Lena stood, leaned in and danced beside Bruno.

It was bizarre watching this petite and talented dancer—dressed in a tight-fitting, clinging black dress—sway alongside the overweight and boyish Bruno. It was actually a little disturbing, and if not for the drugs it would have made no sense.

Lena knelt down and sucked on Bruno's penis. Bruno stopped moving and slowly moaned like a little boy.

"I want her to get paid for that," Susie chimed in, telling Lou.

In some odd way it turned me on watching Lena, someone I found desirable, actually having sex even though it was with the boy-man Bruno.

I looked away and went into the bathroom to wash my face. When I came out, Lena and Bruno were both gone.

Susie looked at me, explaining that they went into separate suites to shower.

* * *

Not long after, I was fighting fatigue sitting in a chair waiting for Lou to tell me what we needed to do next.

Bruno had already dressed and told both of us that he didn't want to go home. The drugs had worn off and he was feeling guilty. He told Lou he'd call him in the morning and left.

Lou was sitting at his desk with envelopes of cash in front of him. Susie, now dressed in an asexual black smock that made her look anything like the madam she was, was reading numbers off of a pad, figuring out how much each girl had earned. Joy was still perky as she did another line of coke on a table in the corner with Elle, who I had hardly had any interaction with. Elle was looking over at Lena, who was asleep curled up in a chair.

"She did 'ludes to come down," Susie told me. She called a car service, woke up Lena and sent her and Joy down to the lobby.

Lou handed her a wad of cash. She quickly looked it over.

"You're generous, Lou," she said.

"Don't mention it," Lou answered.

"You want a blow job?" Susie asked.

"Sure, thanks," Lou answered.

Susie got down on her knees, when Elle belted out a high C as if she was singing opera. We all looked.

"I feel like I am in a Fellini movie," she said. "Hey, you are all invited to my wedding. I want you there, Lou."

Lou made a face and looked at me. "Wacky broad," he said. He sat back and went over his books as Susie blew him. Elle walked to the bathroom and silently waved me over. I followed.

"What's up?" I asked.

"Come in. I want to ask you something," she whispered.

I stepped into the suite's large bathroom and immediately noticed the harsh light. Elle was swaying as she faced me.

"Ask me what?" I asked.

"You carrying?" she asked me.

I didn't answer. She did a line of coke on the huge bathroom counter and got down on her knees. "Be rough with me," she said. "You're the bodyguard. I've been watching you all night. You got a gun on your belt, I know it. It turns me fucking on."

The next thing I knew she undid my zipper.

"Hey," I said stepping back. She was wearing a cute and sexy pink skirt and blouse, which contrasted with her short, very black hair. She looked up at me with her dark eyes and I thought I saw her smile.

"My fiancé is a great guy."

"Does he know you do this?" I asked.

"Oh yeah. He's downstairs right now waiting to take me home. We live in the Bronx. Don't you think I'm hot?"

"Yeah, for sure, but I promised Lou I'd behave myself."

I thought of her on her knees on the tiles in the bathroom with a stranger and with her fiancé waiting downstairs for her in the lobby.

"Pull my hair," she demanded.

"Another time," I told her and quickly exited the bright bathroom.

* * *

NEAR FOUR A.M. I WAS IN the suite with Lou. sitting on one of the large sofas in silence, staring at the half-eaten plates of food and the dozen half-filled glasses that were left behind, decorating the tables and floors as if a banquet had been held and now it was time to digest and sleep.

Lou sat behind the desk with only two remaining envelopes. "Give this one to the security guy. He'll be by in few minutes. His name is Lucas," he said. "And this is yours."

I opened the envelope and glanced at the cash. "It's too much, Lou."

"We're friends. You got enough now to pay off Durrico."

I counted several hundred-dollar bills and pocketed it all. I was drained and spent. I leaned even deeper into the sofa's soft cushion.

"Do you believe that Elle invited me over to her place? The fiancé was downstairs all night waiting for her. Nice looking guy, too. He asked me if he could come up here and mix drinks. He's got to be out of his mind with jealousy, or he gets off on it. Who knows? People are crazy."

Lou glanced at me his tired, dark eyes like an owl's. "I've been calling Rebecca all night. She doesn't pick up."

I could see that he was concerned.

"She go out with a girlfriend?" I asked.

"Who?"

"Then who else could she be with?"

"You tell me," Lou said quizzically getting up. He looked around the room. "I left a nice tip for the maids on the bed. You can crash here. It's all paid for until eleven a.m. checkout time. So's that," he said. He gestured to a short line on the table.

Lou shook my hand and left. I could see his head hanging low as he did.

I sat for a long time in the room alone unable to move.

What did get me to move was the small line of cocaine Lou left for me on the desk. I sat on the chair and looked down at the smooth, glass surface. I didn't even bother with a straw. I put my face down on the table and snorted the line. I felt the hit immediately. I took a deep breath. I picked up the phone and called Nancy.

I heard her voice mumbling. "Who is this?"

"Nancy, it's me. Danny," I said.

There was a moment of silence and I heard her nearly purr. "It's four."

"I want to come over," I told her. There was no way I could have sex with her but I was lonely. I actually just wanted to be with someone who didn't live on the edge like all those I was partying with all night.

"No, she said, sternly.

"I care about you," I told her.

Another few moments of silence passed and she said, "I care about *you*." More silence passed until she hung up the phone.

That one line of cocaine got me out of the suite, out of the hotel, to my car in the garage and all the way back to my apartment in Bayside. The sun was coming up as I collapsed on my bed and fell into a sleep that was more like a trance where I was a phantom, much like some ancient Egyptian visiting the afterlife.

7

As soon as I woke up on Sunday afternoon I called Durrico and told him I had his money for him. All of it. He sounded shocked. We set up a time for me to meet him at Michael's restaurant around seven that night.

I walked into Michael's with the sun setting behind me and found Durrico all alone at a table with one empty chair.

"Rock With You" was playing behind me on the wall speakers. I thought to myself how much I hated that song. I didn't like a lot of the music Michael had "piped" into his restaurant.

I had the cash, mainly in twenties and hundreds, in an envelope. Durrico gestured for me to sit down so I did. I sat and he poured me some wine. He was already halfway through his lasagna. Michael's newspaper was on the far end of the table.

I placed the envelope in front of him, being as discreet as I could. He looked at it and said, "I don't need your money."

I know I clearly had a puzzled look on my face.

"I'm gonna have a big game at my house with some high rollers coming up from AC. I want you to play for me. I'll stake you to that ten grand. But I get twenty percent of the winnings for staking you."

"Fifteen."

He hesitated. "All right—fifteen."

"When?"

"Next Saturday night," he answered. "Be there by eight."

"Okay," I nodded.

"Good," he said.

It was a good deal for me. I played the game and I got to keep eighty-five percent of what I won. He kept the remaining fifteen just for backing me. I kept eighty-five cents on every dollar. It was a good deal for us both. He made money just by staking me because I was a good bet.

I sat back trying to get my bearings. I didn't expect the sudden friendliness when he moved in his chair.

"Tell me about Rebecca."

Now I knew why he was being friendly. "She's Lou's girl."

"I know that part," he said. "What else?"

I saw that Michael was staying away from the table, sitting alone at his own. I nodded to him and turned back to Durrico. "What else *what*?"

"She have anybody in Florida? Boyfriend, husband?"

"Not that I know of."

"She said she was a teacher. You were a teacher. She tellin' the truth?"

"Why not?" I shrugged.

Durrico put down his fork. "How much was Lou into her? According to her, she was only friends with him."

I was quiet.

"You don't buy that?"

"I drove them around. He was staying over. I figure there was something between them, no? Common sense."

Durrico moved the lasagna around on his plate with his fork. "Well, it's all water under the bridge now. She's with me."

"With you?"

"Yeah. At my house in Manhasset. I'm having people pick up her clothes now."

"Lou didn't tell me any of this," I said.

"Lou doesn't know. I want you to tell him."

I looked at the envelope. "And that's worth ten grand to you?"

"Yeah, it is. We're even.

"Why me?"

"Something like this is better comin' from a friend."

I got quiet again. I knew news like this was never good coming from anyone.

"You hungry?" Durrico asked when the waiter appeared.

I ordered scungilli with clam sauce and drank my wine in silence. Durrico probably sensed how uncomfortable I was. He placed his fork on the plate and paid our bill, but before he left the waiter handed him an order of veal scampi to go. "For Rebecca," Durrico said to me to stress the point I didn't want be reminded of. "My house next Saturday night. Come in around eight," he told me, and walked out.

Michael sat down at my table. I filled him in on what had happened and he nodded. "Yeah, he told me before you got here."

He took a deep breath. "This ain't good, this thing with him and this girl Rebecca."

"It's not good," I agreed.

"What does she got that these two guys want her?" Michael asked.

"She's hot."

"Lou will go apeshit," Michael said.

"More than that," I said.

"Greed," Michael said.

"What about it?" I asked.

"The word I was trying to think of to describe what I was talking about the other night. I get this vibe of greed coming out of everyone."

"Okay," I said.

"Greed is the new idealism, Danny. It will be the decade of greed. I have to write a song about that."

I called Lou and drove to his house and waited in the car for him to come out like he wanted me to do. Lou didn't like me seeing his wife and I honestly didn't like being around her either. She always had a lot of questions for me, and most of them I didn't know how to answer.

Lou sat in my car next to me. He was wearing a robe and slippers. "I'm burnt," he said.

"Rebecca is with Durrico, Lou. I met him at Michael's to pay him off and he told me to tell you."

Lou went pale. I never saw him that white before. He didn't move and didn't say anything for what seemed like a real long time. "At his house?"

"Yes," I answered. "He made it sound like she moved in."

I could sense Lou thinking it over, working on a plan, wondering what to do next.

"I'll check the place I rented for her."

"Right," I said. Then I told him about Durrico staking me the ten grand for the game at his place.

"He had that game planned months ago. I guess he wants to show her off," Lou said.

We sat quietly in the car for a few more moments. "I dug her, you know," he said, breaking the silence. "I might have told the wife. I might have given it all up for her."

I kept quiet.

"I can't let him just do this to me," Lou said.

"I know."

Lou sat back and moved in the chair. He hummed to himself the way he did when he was thinking. "Not sure what I'm going to do. One thing I know, it's best to lay low. It's best to wait for Durrico to let his guard down first. When he's thinking it's all over, that's when I'll act," Lou said turning to me, eyeing me with suspicion as he did. "I'm gonna ask you to say something next Saturday at the game. I'm not going but you'll be there and you'll have a second alone with her. I want you to say something. Will you do that for me?"

"Sure."

"Good," Lou said and jumped out of the car, walking briskly back to his house.

I drove home with the uncomfortable feeling that I was being played by both Lou and Durrico, and that there was nothing I could do about it.

* * *

MY ONE SURVIVING RELATIVE WAS MY father's younger sister, my Aunt Leigh. She lived in Valley Stream in a modest ranch-style home with a big backyard right off the Southern State Parkway.

She called me a few times a year mostly around holidays and sometimes out of the blue and that's what she did when

I got home that Sunday night. We spoke briefly and she invited me for dinner on Monday.

My Aunt Leigh was a beauty when she was young and though in her early fifties, she still had the looks. With dark hair that she clearly dyed darker, bright shiny blue eyes and dusky skin, they called her Elizabeth Taylor when she was young, though she really looked like the actress Vivian Leigh who she was named after for that very reason.

She had been married three times, all to either bookies or small-time hoods and now one was dead from being murdered and the other two were doing time in the state prison for loansharking. My Aunt Leigh loved her bad boys.

Her first husband was killed because he was jealous of his own cousin who was sleeping with his wife—my aunt. He went to his cousin's house with gun in hand but his cousin saw him coming and shot him from the side window. His cousin was killed himself in a mob-style hit.

She also had one daughter, Gina, who was born without her mother's looks and driven by the resentment of not being as pretty as her mother. She became a cokehead and was living with a guy somewhere in Toronto who kept her in drugs. My aunt wasn't fond of her daughter.

Sharing our dinner of pot roast and highballs on the small table in her modest kitchen decorated in poor man's art deco in my aunt's one-floor house, I shared with my only living relative who I spoke to, the truth of my situation—why I left teaching, why I was writing a novel about her father, my grandfather, how I was living off my poker winnings, and how I met a girl I really liked.

My aunt listened because she wanted me to believe she was concerned. She was no saint and though she was living off cash left to her by her crazy husbands and the small salary she was paid from a part-time job she had in an accounting office, I knew she was hard as nails and wasn't above asking for a handout from me since she had several times in the past. I always obliged with whatever I had.

The guy she worked for was married but was obsessed with my aunt, so he kept her working even though half the time he didn't really need her and most of the time he just wanted her to be near him. I figured she had sex with him once in a while to keep her job and keep him at bay. I met him once. There was absolutely nothing attractive about him at all, and all of my aunt's men had been sexy and dangerous in their time.

My Aunt Leigh seduced me once when I was twelve years old. She was babysitting and walked in on me masturbating. Instead of running out of the room, she sat on the bed next to me. She was smiling as if it were all a joke, ignoring my complete humiliation. I had an open *Playboy* on the bed and she closed it. "Does your mother know you do this?" she asked.

My mother had a drinking problem and eventually died in a car accident when I was twenty-six but even then, while growing up, I hardly saw her. My father was a tough guy who wasn't as tough as he thought. When confronted by his friend, who was sleeping with my mother, he ran away. "He should have shot them both dead," my aunt once told me. He ran off to Mexico and after a couple of years remarried and disappeared again. I had heard nothing from him since the day he ran off.

But that night she walked in on me and caught me masturbating, my aunt, sitting next to me on the bed, put her hand on my thigh and said that I was doing it all wrong and proceeded to show me how it should be done.

I didn't feel seduced; in fact, I felt grateful that she was interested enough to do what she did. After I came all over her hands, she got up and went to the bathroom and washed herself. She came back into the room and stood at the open door. "Pleasure isn't bad; just don't become obsessed with it."

She left the room and continued her babysitting task by inviting a boyfriend over. I could hear them moaning all night on the sofa.

Though we saw one another through the years, we never discussed the events of that night. She never touched me again and I never mentioned it. She would occasionally call me "sexy" and I'd tell her she was "hot" and that was the extent of our flirting.

"Life runs you down," she said to me. She was wearing some kind of lacy white collar over a dark blue blouse and a dark blue skirt just a little too tight for her expanding hips. "It sounds like you like hanging with these tough guys too much. Just like your father did."

"I want to write a book about grandpa," I told her.

"That's a nice gesture. He was a tough guy too."

Most of the night went by with her telling me stories about my mother and father and how they met, how they married and how they fought. My aunt never held back, giving me the blow by blow of their courtship and my birth as if they were the details of some catastrophe. In her telling of it, I was the byproduct of their tragic love story and neither really wanted me.

"But you were some hottie even as a little boy," my aunt told me. "And you loved climbing trees and falling down.

What you didn't do to get that rush. You still like that rush, don't you?" she said.

My aunt didn't do cocaine but she loved her highballs and as I sipped mine she slugged down hers. Eventually she told me that being lonely was a part of life. "Nobody gets out of life alive," was her favorite saying.

Before I left somewhere near eleven, since she had to work the next morning, she asked me if I had any extra money lying around for her. I was expecting her to ask.

"I got a big game coming up this weekend. If all goes well, I'll bring you some of my winnings," I told her.

When I was leaving she kissed me on the lips like she always did when we left one another. "My only living relative," she'd say, completely ignoring the fact that she had a daughter and I always knew it was better never to mention that she did.

8

Durrico's card game started out as a party. Durrico loved to be the center of attention. I arrived at his house in Manhasset and left my car with the valet parking attendant waiting at the top of a long winding driveway to the front door flanked by white pillars.

I stepped into the lobby and found myself greeted by a waiter who quickly picked me out and led me through the house, which was decorated with white furniture and Roman-like statues and, oddly enough, abstract paintings. The floors were polished wood and everywhere you looked there were little ashtrays filled with white powder.

I recognized some faces in the room. The men and women were tanned from a weekend in Miami or the Islands and most were in pretty good shape.

There were around forty people in the house, of which I figured only half would be playing, and when the waiter led me outside to the backyard I saw two poker tables set up under a large tent. Each table fit ten players.

The backyard included a lit swimming pool and a mani-cured green lawn. I went to a small bar at the far corner under the tent and asked for a scotch and soda, spun around and saw Rebecca. She was standing with Durrico, who was wearing a perfectly pressed white short-sleeved shirt and pleated black pants. He nodded to me and I nodded back. Rebecca gave me an odd, friendly smile.

"You're probably the second best player in the room," Durrico said to me.

"Who's the first?" I asked.

"Me," he said.

Rebecca stepped over to us. "Hello, Danny," she said.

"Hello, Rebecca." She was wearing a sleek dark blue dress with her breasts inching their way out of it just enough to make you stare and just enough for you to want to see more.

"Nice, huh?" Durrico said to me, nodding to what I thought were her breasts but he was actually bringing atten-tion to a beautiful emerald necklace she was wearing.

"Charlie bought it for me," she smiled. "I like mixing blue and green."

"Blue and green can go nice," I said.

Durrico laughed this very genuine, loud laugh. I knew he thought it funny that I was staring at her breasts when he gestured to the necklace.

* * *

I SAT AT ONE TABLE AND Durrico at another and in a couple of hours we were both the big winners. The high rollers like the rush of gambling but never took the time to do the hard work, studying the other players and how they played, and they had no patience. The minute they had a pair they were raising. It was easy pickings for the entire night.

What was difficult was getting alone with Rebecca. I saw my chance when Durrico was in a big hand at his table. I took a bathroom break and on my way from the restroom I saw Rebecca in the dinning room speaking to one of the other women. I waved her over and was surprised when she came.

"Lou wanted me to say he has no grudge with you. He also said he got the mother-of-pearl earrings he promised for you," I told her.

"He should give them to his wife," she said.

"He wants you to have them. When you get a minute just call him and he said he'll set up a time and place for me to hand them to you," I told her.

"He doesn't have to go through all that trouble," Rebecca said coolly.

"They're expensive. And he wants you to have them for all the good times," I said, then quickly turned and went back to my table where I proceeded to go up ten grand.

By the end of the night Durrico and I were the big winners. I gave him his fifteen percent cut, shook his hand and left.

I went home with my pockets full and the message for Lou from Rebecca. Just before I left she walked by me and whispered as she did, "Tell Lou I'll call."

* * *

THE NEXT DAY I CALLED LOU to tell him that Rebecca said she'd call him and he was happy to hear that. I took my winnings and spent the next few days picking up cash at a few small games. In the middle of the week Lou called and told me to meet him at Visage.

We sat at our usual place at the bar and Lou ordered a bottle of Moët despite the silly conversation with Durrico on what was better. "She called," he said sharing with me the details. "She's all heart that one. She wants the mother-of-pearl earrings. She probably thinks they are antiques but they're not."

I listened closely.

"She's playing me for an asshole," he said. "She knows I got it big for her."

"When are you going to see her?"

"You're going to pick her up for me early Saturday morning. Durrico is playing golf. She'll have a few hours. I'll tell you where to bring her when I figure it out," he said.

"Lou, I really don't want to get involved anymore," I said and meant it. "I did you the favor. Now it's between the two of you."

Lou poured me another glass. "I understand but I was there for you."

"I know you were."

Lou lowered his jaw, leaned in toward me. "Just pick her up for me and drop her off. She won't see me any other way," he said. "She trusts you."

My silence was my way of agreeing, though I felt uncomfortable about it.

Around two a.m. we went to the diner on Tenth Avenue and were sitting at a booth near the window talking about things when I noticed four Spanish guys standing outside the window making faces at us.

"You know them?" I asked.

Lou looked, said "No" and went back to his burger.

We continued to talk and the four Spanish guys continued eyeing us. They were in their twenties, wearing sports jackets and were sharing a joint and a beer bottle that clearly had something stronger in it than beer.

At some point they started laughing and pointing to us. They were near the front door and we'd have to go by them to get to Lou's car.

I finished my cheeseburger and milkshake and Lou got the check. "You carrying?" he asked.

"No."

He nodded. We got up, paid the cashier and walked out.

"You two faggots?" one of the Spanish guys asked.

Lou took a few steps with me at his side. He stopped when he felt they were all in front of him and turned. I turned with him. All four stood in the harsh blue neon light. Half the sign was busted and dark but the part that was working blasted the word "diner" into the surrounding darkness. The two guys closest to us and were clearly the leaders.

"You said what?" Lou asked.

"I said you two look like some real nice faggots," he said. "You punks like to kiss?" The one to his left nodded as he said that.

Lou stepped closer to the one who spoke and slowly reached into his jacket pocket. He didn't say a word but inched closer.

"So, you carrying?" the guy asked.

Lou continued to stay quiet. I now slowly came at the other side of the second guy, watching his two friends behind him slowly back away.

All four of them were so stoned their eyes looked orange to me in the harsh blue neon sign. They slowly bounced back and forth, putting the weight of one foot on the other, with their heads bobbing up and down like buoys in the river.

Everything went still. No one moved. I was about to turn around and walk back to the car when Lou pulled out his automatic pistol, swung it around and cracked the guy who was doing all the talking across the forehead.

I heard the smack of metal on skull and saw blood pour out. Lou hit the guy again across the bridge of his nose with blood shooting out straight up in the air. The guy let out a moan as if his head was filled with air and now it was all being released by the contact with the pistol.

"Fuck, I got blood on my shirt sleeve," Lou said as calmly as if it was an everyday occurrence. He turned and walked back to the parking lot, ignoring everything that transpired. I stepped back, hearing myself cringe with an odd sound as I watched the guy Lou had just hit crumple to the ground face forward on the sidewalk.

I turned and calmly walked back to the car with Lou. He opened the doors to his caddie and in seconds we were pulling out of the parking lot.

"You get your guy?"

"Huh?" I asked incredulously.

Lou drove up on the sidewalk, flooring the car and hitting the one closest to the guy he had just hit, clipping him on the knee with his fender knocking him backward. "There goes a kneecap," he said as he drove up Tenth Avenue and made a left crosstown toward the Queensboro Bridge.

"Koch better do something about the street crime or this whole fucking city is going to be like Friday the 13th," was the only thing he said all the way home. And he didn't even hum.

9

"WHERE ARE YOU TAKING ME?" REBECCA asked when she got into my car and got into the back seat as a matter of habit.

"Lou said to take you to his office," I answered.

"Why his office?"

"Nobody's there today. His wife's home. I guess it's the best place and you won't be long," I answered.

Rebecca climbed in next to me. Just her sitting there in silence close enough for me to touch made me realize why these two guys were fighting over her. She was one of those women who had a natural sexiness about them. She was sensual and confident and she exuded both qualities and the kind of men I knew loved that. We drove on in silence for the first part of the BQE but eventually she opened up.

"I figure what you think of me."

"I don't think anything, Rebecca," I told her. "You did what you did."

"What did I do?" she asked accusingly.

"You dumped Lou for Charlie. That's between the three of you, not me, so who cares what I think?"

"I care what you think."

"Why?"

"You're a smart guy," Rebecca told me. "You're different than them. I'm not what you think I am. I can tell the difference between a guy like you and a guy like them."

I stayed quiet.

"I'm not a whore."

I continued to keep quiet.

"Charlie has his doubts that I am and Lou is sure I am," she said wistfully. "Don't go to Lou's."

"What?"

"Let's go somewhere," she told me.

"Go where?"

"Your place," she said without a touch of anything in her voice other than sincerity.

Though surprised, I did entertain the thought, but I knew if I took her to my apartment she'd take one look around and leave. It wasn't what she was used to. "You'd hate my place."

"Try me. I'm a simple girl."

I astonished myself and thought long and hard about the notion but in the end I realized that even if she stayed for the night she'd get bored. She wasn't that kind of woman. She needed high-powered guys and high-powered toys. I was and had neither. I also knew that Lou would be more than just annoyed if I didn't show up with her. "I'm confused here," I told her.

"Don't be. I have no interest in the mother-of-pearl earrings. I just wanted to see you," she said. She put her hand on my leg. "Find a phone. Tell Lou I didn't show."

I drove down along the BQE and drove past the Meeker/Morgan Exit. When I got to Brooklyn Heights I got back on the BQE to the Long Island Expressway and I got off the Utopia Parkway exit. A gas station on the corner had a pay phone that I'd use once in a while. "You sure?" I asked.

"I have to get back in a few hours. Charlie is coming home for dinner," she said looking relieved.

I put a quarter in the phone and called Lou. "She wasn't there," I lied.

I could hear him on the phone also sounding slightly relieved. "Okay, thanks."

I hung up and sat back down. She put her hand on my leg again. "How far do you live from here?"

"Not far," I answered and drove off.

When we got to my building and I opened the door for her I sensed how out of place she was in my neighborhood. Her elegance stood out in the midst of working mothers and immigrant families.

I rushed her in through the lobby and into the elevator as if embarrassed by her and she noticed. "I embarrass you or something?"

"Why do you say that?" I asked hoping the elevator wouldn't stop as we went up to the sixth floor.

She leaned in and kissed me gently on the lips. The doors opened and a middle-aged Colombian couple I knew slightly stepped in, all dressed for their Saturday shopping. They both took one look at Rebecca and she smiled at them as the elevator continued to the sixth floor. We both got out and the coupled stayed in and went back down.

I took out my key and opened the door, letting Rebecca in and closing the door behind me.

Once in the apartment I sat on the bed. My apartment looked and felt small once she stepped inside. She looked around indifferently and sat on the bed next to me.

"Now I got two big shots on my bad side," I said.

"What do you mean?" Rebecca asked.

"Lou would kill me if he knew I took you here. And Charlie would do the same. I'm out of my mind, aren't I?" I said rhetorically.

I turned to Rebecca and she looked like a sublime chiseled statue in the sunlight easing through my shades. We were in a shadow and the air was cool enough that I could keep the windows closed.

We kissed. She moved her lips to under my earlobe and said, working her way back to my mouth, "I have some coke."

I nodded. She pulled out a vial from her pocketbook. I quickly grabbed a book from the shelf and laid it on the bed. She made a line and I grabbed two clean straws from the kitchen and ran back to the bed.

We did two lines each. I felt the power of the powder when I reached over and undid the blouse of the magnificent creature across from me. In seconds her breasts, neat and pointed, soft and showing exquisite tan lines, were in my face.

She moaned as I sucked on her tits, putting her hand on my head, pushing me to her chest. "More," she said, and I watched her through one eye as she touched herself, reaching for my penis with her other hand.

I stood up to pull down my pants when she grabbed my penis and put my cock on the tip of her tongue and started licking it. I shivered, jerked back as she sucked my penis.

I wanted to undress her but I couldn't move. The pleasure she was giving me made me an immobile prisoner and the cocaine was stalling any possibility of my having rational thoughts.

I reached for her but she kept me at a distance as if she were a lioness placating my desires for her own recreation.

When you have sex on cocaine you stay hard, but the pleasure intensifies until your penis actually becomes numb. It feels as if all the blood in your body is rushing to your penis and your brain is being hotwired by shocks of electrical impulses. You no longer feel human. You lose the ability to reflect and string together more than one coherent thought at a time. You're euphoric.

Rebecca stood, pushing me back on the bed. She quickly pulled off her blouse and slid out of her slacks. She was naked and stood over me as if I were prey. Because of the shadows, I couldn't make out all of her features, but I could see how elegant she was despite the hardboiled edge and the mercenary spirit. She licked her fingers and touched her vagina, working to make it wet. I figured some women might dry up from the coke despite the necessity to fuck.

She grabbed my penis and when it was stiff enough she put one perfectly manicured foot on the bed next to me and squatted on top and pushed down. We moaned in unison and over and over again she pumped her hips down over me until she was fully lubricated.

Up and down she went, sliding down to my testicles and up to the tip of my penis without our hands or lips touching. We were fucking in the best definition of the word and all I could do was take her in: her magnificent mane of hair, the smell of her tanned and pampered upper body and the tiny beads of sweat forming on her hips and well-tanned belly.

She had her eyes closed, concentrating on the thrusting of our pelvises, working to make them become one with one purpose, in unison, and that was to force the sensations we were experiencing to the breaking point. "Don't come yet!" she demanded.

I was amazed that she had known I was getting close.

"Not yet," she said.

"Okay," I told her. I put my hands on her hips to do the best I could to slow down her thrusts, allowing her to pinpoint that spot she seemed desperate to find.

"Grab my hair," she told me.

I reached up and took her hair in both hands.

"Pull back," she ordered. "Pull my hair back." She took my right hand, placing it on her breasts. "Squeeze my nipples harder! Harder!" she told me until I squeezed hard enough that she moaned again but this time I could hear in that moan she was getting closer to her own orgasm.

"Are you ready?" she said, nearly out of breath.

"Yes," I said. I had been holding back, doing all I could not to cum until she did. When she shoved her hips deep into mine and let out scream of release I finally caved in and orgasmed as well. And as she was having hers, she grabbed my testicles right at their most sensitive place, making me jerk up and shoot all the sperm I had into her with my own ferocious explosion of carnal sensation.

I felt her body tremble with mine and felt as if all the energy in the room had been placed in one molecule of matter, which was our bodies releasing the energy into the universe of my room.

In a matter of moments she slowly lay face forward over me. I felt the sweat from her nearly perfectly textured flesh touching mine. I put my hands on her tight ass, allowing her to sigh and breathe as if she were a part of me.

"That was nice," she said. She rolled over me and I was still trying to accept how this beauty was in my apartment, naked on my bed. "I like you because you're smart." She reached over and turned on my radio. She kept turning the knob, leaning over on her side, giving me a great view of her back as it sloped in a perfect symmetrical line to her hips. She stopped turning the knob with "Magic" by The Cars playing and leaned back to me.

"You like me because I'm smart. Not because I'm rich and tough," I said.

"Lou and Charlie have money, but I know rich. I was dating a drug dealer from Brazil who had a yacht ten stories high and a mansion in Rio. He'd take me all around the islands," she told me.

"Cool life for a high school teacher," I smiled and hugged her.

She edged closer. "He got bored of me. So, I went back to teaching. I loved teaching but that sucked too, but not for the reasons you'd expect. There wasn't a day that went by that I wasn't hit on by other teachers, principals, students, men and women. I got tired of it. I figured let me play in the big game if that's how it was going to be. So I try," she told me.

"Lou is the big game?"

"He got me to New York."

"And Charlie?" I asked.

"I like Charlie but it's time to move on. I didn't know there was such bad blood between those two. I want no part of small-time "hate games." I'm thinking Europe. I met this guy the other day in Manhattan. I was shopping at Bloomingdale's. He wants to take me to Rome. I think I'm going," she said and started getting dressed.

"Well, thanks for stopping by," I said.

She leaned in and kissed me softly on the lips. "You might be a big deal writer some day. I want to say I was *with* you," she smiled. "I wanted to write once. But it was only a phase. My writing is so bad I can't even keep a journal."

An hour later I was dropping her off at a small mall a few blocks from Durrico's house in Manhasset. She put on her sunglasses and waved goodbye, walking off into the sunshine. Driving home I realized I liked her a lot more than I ever thought possible.

I spent the rest of the day writing my book, went to Michael's to have dinner but he had left early so I went home and near dusk I found the vial of cocaine Rebecca had brought with her. She had left the remains with me. I spent the next hour with one eye on the vial and making several trips to the phone, wanting to call Nancy but stopping myself every time. Exhausted from writing a first draft of an entire chapter I treated myself to a hit of the coke and drove to Visage by myself.

The usual Saturday night faces filled the place and I found a seat at the bar, sipped my scotch, listened to the music and saw the ghosts of Lou and Durrico everywhere I looked. I also thought it was a good alibi in case Lou thought something was up with me. Here I was alone at Visage.

I felt uneasy that it was Saturday night and neither had shown up. I felt a wave of loneliness wash over me and I fought it, smiling at every pretty face I saw but not connecting to any of them. It was near eleven when I saw Nancy with her date and I figured it had to be the lawyer Brian.

They must have come in when I was in the bathroom or walking around. They were sitting at a table off the bar, not in the most desirable spot, and I saw that she purposely faced me. It didn't take me long to figure she brought him to Visage in hopes of running into me. I went with the concept as long as I could until I eventually walked over to their table.

"Hey, Nancy," I said.

"Hi, Danny," she smiled and introduced me to Brian, who asked me to sit. In a few minutes I was ordering a bottle of champagne. "Chandon," I said. Nancy smiled.

I let Brian talk and he did. He sounded like a lawyer, making sure he was precise in his thoughts, clear in his pronunciation but all the while sounding completely dull. He was a commercial properties attorney and wanted to talk about the rise of commercial property sales in Nassau County. I smiled and nodded at everything he said without taking my eyes off of Nancy.

Eventually, Nancy excused herself to go to the ladies' room, leaving Brian and me alone.

I had the vial burning a hole in my pocket. I waited a few seconds and excused myself.

I pushed myself into the ladies' room and a tall blond woman doing her makeup glared at me. "Ladies' room, buddy," she said.

I quickly searched the stalls and saw Nancy's shoes. I pushed it open. She was taking a piss but when I barged in she smiled. I quickly closed the stall door behind me and took out a straw I had in my jacket pocket and poured a line on the back of my hand.

With her stockings and panties down around her ankles she did the hit and I kissed her just as she threw her head back from the rush. She stuck her tongue into my mouth and we kissed like two demons that had been locked away from one another for too long a period of time and now were back together.

She grabbed my crotch but I was soft. I had trouble getting hard. "What's wrong?" Nancy asked.

"Nothing," I said, trying to finger her to get her mind off my limp penis. I quickly felt how wet she was. The coke was numbing me up.

The blond had called a security guard who banged on the stall. Nancy pulled up her underclothing and we ran out of the ladies' room hand in hand.

"Let's ditch Brian," I said.

Nancy rushed past me and we raced down the stairs and out of Visage.

We went back to my car and did the entire vial of coke and kissed furiously like two fugitives on the run. She pushed her nipples in my face and I made her cum just by doing that, all the while keeping my pants on.

I started the car and sped away and while driving down the West Side Highway I tossed the empty vial out of the car. Nancy was flying like a demon, taking in the mass of lights and images as she stuck her face out the window as "Heartache Tonight" was blasting on the car radio.

She turned to me as I drove over the nearly empty Brooklyn Bridge and grabbed my crotch again squeezing it hard. She took it out of my pants and sucked on it and I came before we got to Brooklyn.

I took her back to my apartment and she put all the lights on in the place and wanted to talk. We were both coked out, so the conversation was the most important thing in our lives. Nancy told me how she wanted to some day get married, have a family and live in a nice ranch-style house. She had seen one she liked over in Garden City that had stayed in her mind for years.

For some reason talking about Long Island made me think of my aunt who I had forgotten to call.

We did another line and talked about where our lives were and what we wanted to do. We talked about how we were nearly at the mid-point of our existence and that everything we did mattered in some way, shaping our future. It was all drug talk. Our minds were racing and our thoughts were being thrown out into the universe as if they had some purpose.

I opened the windows and watched the sun come up and somewhere in there Nancy collapsed onto my bed.

I crawled in next to her and neither of us moved an inch until sometime near four.

My phone was ringing and I answered it with no voice. I had to cough several times to be heard. But I did recognize the voice on the other end.

"I need you, Danny. I got a serious problem," Lou said.

Lou asked me to meet him at his office. It was already late afternoon. I agreed.

Nancy got on her clothes, looking drained. "I have school tomorrow," she said.

"I'll drive you home."

On the drive Nancy held my hand. I took a few glances at her and I could see how depleted she looked. She squeezed my hand and shook her head. "What do we have?"

"Excuse me?"

"We have drugs and sex, Danny. Not much else."

I had no idea we were going to have a serious conversation. I was not in the mood for one.

When we arrived at her apartment she looked at me with the same sad puppy dog eyes I saw the night before from Brian. "Are you going to call me?" she asked.

"You know I am. After I see Lou. When I get home," I told her.

She got out and I quickly turned the car around and drove to Lou's office in Williamsburg.

10

I GOT TO LOU'S OFFICE ON Meeker and parked on the street. I had stopped at a diner for a coffee and I still had the Styrofoam cup in my hand when Lou let me through the metal gates.

He now had a Doberman in the back chained to a fence near the far end of the truck lot. Several dump trucks sat in a row and you could see the Doberman was excited to see someone new show up at the office so he barked like crazy.

Lou turned his back on me and quickly led me into his office, pulling down the shade after he closed the door behind us. We stood face to face in the translucent light from his one large office light bulb.

I noticed that Lou was sweating profusely and I could see lines of coke on his table. "Do a hit," he said.

I leaned down and snorted a line right off the table without a straw. I was still shaky from the night before and the coffee just wasn't doing it so a hit was just the right remedy to get me straight.

Lou did a line and led me into the back room, which was where he kept a lot of spare parts for the trucks and earthmovers he repaired and sold.

"Where we going?" I asked.

"Hold on," he answered.

Everything was made of metal and dusty. I edged past steal buckets and boxes on the floor filled with nails and drill bits and industrial tools.

"Watch your step," Lou said as he led me deeper into his office where the windows were closed tight and whitewashed so no one could look in or out.

He pushed open a metal door that was jammed tight and we walked deeper into a storage room. "Get in," he said, his voice cracking.

I edged in right behind him and he shoved the door shut. It was pitch black inside. I was about to say something when he reached up to the overhead light and pulled the string. It took a few seconds for my eyes to adjust.

I was perplexed as to why Lou had brought me here. I could only see wooden crates filled with metal filings, old engine parts and shelves lined with rusted tools.

Lou stepped to my right and stared down at a corner of the room. I saw something large wrapped in plastic lying on a white sheet.

"We had a fight. She smacked me hard." He placed the side of his right hand on the left side of his face where I saw a long, deep scratch, still red, right under his left eye, which I hadn't noticed before. "I didn't mean to hit her that hard, Danny. I just lost it, you know. I punched her hard on the jaw. Just once, man. She fell back and hit her head on that metal table I have in the front room. She just went limp. Just like that," he said. "And she was high, really high."

He moved to the plastic and slowly unraveled it. It was Rebecca under it, lying there motionless, pale, her head without a scratch on it. No blood, no bruises. Her mane of hair was covering her forehead. She didn't even look dead to me.

She was dressed in something different than when I had seen her last. She was wearing an orange blouse and black pants. She was still in her heels and I could still see the facial makeup.

I stepped closer and leaned back against a tall wooden stool to get a better look. "Fuck," I said.

"Yeah," he replied.

"When did it happen?"

"She met me here around nine. Durrico went to the Bronx to see someone and so she called me. She took a cab to Union Street and I met her and drove her over here."

I could see now that her eyes were circled black and her nose bent to the right. Lou was left-handed.

"You only hit her once?" I asked.

"Just once. But she was wearing those heels, you see, and she fell back on that metal piece there. It must have hit the one soft spot in her skull. I don't know? I have been sitting here trying to figure it all out. She hit her head hard, Danny, and with all the coke in her, who knows? I think she was high all last night it seemed. It was an accident," Lou explained.

I was wondering why she had gone to see him when she had told me that she wasn't all that interested anymore in either him or Durrico or the antique mother-of-pearls earrings.

"She got me really mad, Danny. She said she met some guy and was going off to Europe with him. She said that she didn't really want to deal with the bad blood between me and Durrico."

I still couldn't figure why Rebecca took the chance to see Lou if she didn't have to, unless she had lied to me and the earrings did matter to her.

"I have to get rid of her," Lou said, staring down at the body.

"Rid of her?"

"Yeah. I can keep her here for a little while since no one comes back here and nobody has the keys but me. Plus I got the dog to keep people away. But you gotta help me move her," he told me.

"Lou, this is like a homicide, man. I mean, I know it's an accident, sure, but it's still manslaughter."

Lou didn't react to the obvious. Instead, he covered Rebecca up and sat on a very small wooden stool behind me. He folded his hands in his lap. "She used me, Danny."

"She was with Durrico. You should have left her alone."

"I couldn't. She was under my skin. Just her being here made me want to have her. That was why we had the fight. I touched her and she pushed me away," he told me.

"She really came for the mother-of-pearl?"

"Who the fuck knows why she came?" he answered.

I stepped back hoping some options would come to me. I knew that I couldn't just leave her and pretend I never saw her, though I could take a chance that Lou would never mention that I was here. I could call the police but I'd be implicating myself and knowing the cops they would build a story of jealousy and somehow involve me in the murder. I knew how they worked hearing enough of the stories from guys on the street.

They would put pressure on me to rat out not only Lou but once they figured out what I knew, they'd want more information from me about Lou and people like Durrico and who they got their coke from. All I had to do was give one name and that would be the end of me. The homicide guys would hand me over to the vice guys and in no time I'd wind up like Rebecca, lying dead in somebody's back room waiting to be made to disappear with my body being hacked by Colombians like Lenny "The Roach" or wise guys like Durrico and Lou who all shared secrets.

The only other option was to help Lou out.

An hour later we were sitting in the Sage Diner on Queens Boulevard. I was sipping some coffee and munching slowly on a bagel with butter as Lou just stared at his coffee cup.

The inane "Upside Down" played on the table jukebox. Lou slammed it off.

There were a few people at booths and tables scattered around us. Lou was sullen yet strangely enough not as panic-stricken as I was, considering we were discussing how to hide Rebecca's corpse.

"The Florida cops are going to start looking for her once her parents don't hear from her. They will know I flew her up here I'm guessing, since she told them everything she did," Lou said. "I am thinking there is no way I can hide her. Down the line NYPD is going to check everything I own. My house, my business properties. Everything," he said.

"You thought this out," I said, feeling uneasy and troubled.

"I have had nothing to think about since," he said. "The good thing is nobody but you can trace her to seeing me. Durrico is in the dark, I have to figure."

"What about the guy she was going to Europe with?" I asked.

"I don't know his name. She mention it to you?"

"Nope."

Lou got quiet. "Maybe she made him up. Either way, even if he is real, we have to take the chance he left for Europe by now," Lou said.

"Right," I answered.

"So, whatever we do we make this trail really hard to follow. But we have to put her somewhere nobody will figure on."

"They can connect me to her through you," I said.

Lou nodded. "You drove for me. You picked her up at the airport but your connection to her ends when she moved in with Charlie. The cops will haunt Charlie and not you or me."

Outside the diner we stood by his car for a few minutes allowing the night and its presence to weigh down on us. The lights, the sounds of cars driving by, the silences in between were anything but soothing.

"What do you think about my boat?" he asked.

"Taking her body out into the bay?" I asked.

"Yeah," he answered. "I know the dock is crowded this time of year. I know they will check the boat as part of my property. I know we'd have to explain why we went out that late and that far if we get seen," he said talking himself out of that possibility.

"I don't know, Lou," I said.

"Think of a place where nobody can connect you and me. Someplace they'd never look for the body. Someplace no judge would ever give them a warrant to dig up or search through and if you can come up with something, we're home free," Lou said. "But come up with a place fast." He got into his car and drove off.

I stood alone in the lot, thinking. The one thing that bothered me above all else was that I wasn't sure how much Lou knew about me being with Rebecca. Maybe she told him and that's why he hit her. Lou was sharp and he knew it was better not to tell me what he knew until he had my help. He played his cards well. That is how these guys survived on the street: they played their hands like surgeons. Then I thought of my Aunt Leigh.

* * *

MY AUNT LEIGH, WEARING HER LIGHT blue housecoat and blue slippers with bunny rabbits on them, took the cash from me. It was only a few hundred but she hungrily folded it and placed it in her purse. Her hair was pulled back in a pony-tail, hoping to get the effect that she was a teenager even though her teen days were light years into the past.

I sat across the kitchen table from her and could see the sky spraying golden light through the window on the door that led to the backyard. The glaring light just missed shining in my face.

I glimpsed through the window the small wooden shack in the corner of her backyard, which was pretty much hidden from view from the surrounding neighbors.

"So that's the whole story," I said. "Lou and this other guy wore masks and ripped off this Colombian drug dealer. Now they need a place to hide the drugs."

"And that's the whole story?" my aunt asked.

"*All* of it," I replied.

"How much is this Lou willing to pay me?"

"How much do you want?" I asked.

"How much are the drugs worth on the street?" she asked.

"A lot," I told her.

"To hide stolen drugs in my shack? Five grand up front," she answered.

I had lied to my aunt. I knew that the truth was the best lie.

"I am thinking that there's a good reason you came to me. Probably no drug dealers are going to think of looking at my place for drugs you stole. So, five grand in cash. How long does he need to keep it there?"

"Not sure," I answered.

"Five grand for now. If it stays in there longer than I want it to, I want five more, got that?"

"I got it," I told her.

"I'm driving down to AC for a couple of days. I'll call you when I am down there. You two put the drugs in there when I'm away. That way I never knew a thing. I never met this guy Lou. Never. You got that?"

"Yes."

"Or I will turn the both of you rat bastards in. You leave the cash in the house after you are done. You place one envelope with twenties and fifties upstairs."

"Where upstairs?"

"Follow me," she said. "I'll show you."

My Aunt Leigh led me to the bathroom and got down on one knee and put her head under the clothes hamper that was built into the wall. "Get down," she said.

I did. She took my hand and I felt a hole in the wall underneath the hamper. "You push the envelope in deep."

"Right," I said.

"I'll leave the key under the mat in front of the shack."

We walked back to the front door. We stood facing one another in silence for a long awkward moment.

She closed the door on me before I could say anything else.

11

As I waited for my aunt to call to let me know that she was in AC, I hung out with Lou, and when I wasn't with him, I was hustling poker games. I was on a losing streak and it was screwing up my confidence. When I wasn't playing, I was at Michael's complaining about my streak and Michael was telling me about how the eighties had only just started but he didn't like the start at all.

"I want to go back in time," he said.

"You can't," I told him.

"I'm going to be a father," he said. "Lillian is pregnant."

"It's what you want," I said.

"I don't want a kid of mine growing up in a world we got now. I want a world filled with good vibrations," he said. "Just like Brian Wilson wrote."

"Sounds good," I said.

When I wasn't with Michael, I was hanging out with Lou getting high and doing all I could not to talk about our situation with Rebecca.

Eventually my Aunt Leigh called to tell me that she was

going to Atlantic City. I got on the phone and told Lou to put our plan in motion. My aunt took a bus down to AC and that night, Lou and I met at his office and wrapped Rebecca's body in a large dark carpet Lou had picked up and slid her into the bed of his dump truck.

Up to that moment we did lines of cocaine in his office while he answered calls like he did every night dealing with his trucks, dump sites and business deals on his construction machinery. We wanted everything to look as it usually did.

Somewhere near eleven we drove out to Valley Stream and once we got the key, finding it under the mat where my aunt said it would be, we got into the house using only flashlights to find our way. We opened the shack door and spent several hours digging a hole in the ground. We were sweating bullets not only from the physical exertion but also from the coke we continued to do to give us strength.

We both knew it was a working-class neighborhood, meaning that most of the people who lived there had day jobs and worked, so we were counting on that fact helping us not be seen.

Lou also picked up some Black Beauties for us to do to keep us awake and to give us plenty of energy. We also brought along a big gallon of water—which we drank from constantly.

Once the hole was dug, we waited until around two and eased Rebecca out of the trunk and carried her in through the house into the backyard. We both wore black T-shirts and overalls Lou bought for us to better blend into the night.

The house on the right was our only concern. Someone in the house had a bedroom light on all night and though we wanted to wait for it to go out we eventually decided to gamble and make the move.

Once Rebecca was in the shack, we cut open the rug and removed the plastic. We were hit with an awful stench but were prepared with hospital masks, which Lou had gotten for us and they helped a little.

We slid Rebecca's decaying remains feet first into the hole and quickly filled it in with all the dirt in the shack. It was a tight place to work in—so tight we were sometimes unable to actually move with the shovels.

It was getting close to dawn when we patted down the last of the earth. Our plan was to get it all done in one night so as not to create suspicion. Unfortunately the sun came up earlier and we had a lot to do before it was up.

Once we patted down the last mound of earth and placed the blanket over Rebecca's grave, we leaned up against the shack's back wall and sipped the remaining water. We spoke only in whispers.

"You said that Rebecca stood you up that day, huh?" Lou asked. "But she didn't stand you up, did she?" he said, his voice dropping, his dark, chocolate brown eyes ripping into mine.

I frowned.

"She told me about you two. We were fighting and it came out. She told me she was at your place Saturday and you two fucked your brains out, right? You lied to me. She was nothing to you and you were nothing to her but a fuck, but she was a lot to me, man." Lou took a deep breath. "Did anyone see you two together?" Lou asked.

"What do you mean?" I asked.

"The afternoon you two were together," he said.

I thought of the Colombian couple that saw me and Rebecca in the elevator.

"Did anyone see you two together?" he asked again.

"Maybe," I said.

"When?"

"When she came up to my apartment," I told him.

He took my hand and held it. "You fucked her behind my back, friend. I'll never understand that."

I let go of Lou's hand. "She came on to me, Lou. I know it's no excuse but that was the kind of woman she was. She came on to Durrico, she had this new guy who was taking her to Europe, nobody could say 'no' to her. She was that special."

Lou took in what I had just said. "We're done here. Let's go."

I felt uneasy but agreed that we were done.

Once back in the pickup, he handed me the five grand in cash and I went back into the house, placing it exactly under the clothes hamper in the wall.

We drove back to Brooklyn with Lou humming "Working My Way Back to You" off-key all the way there. We drove into his shop yard and closed all the doors.

Lou poured disinfectant all around where Rebecca's corpse had been laying all that time and we cut up the plastic she had been wrapped in and he burned it right there in the far backroom, one piece at a time.

Still flying from the speed pills, we were filthy with sweat. Lou reached into a drawer in his desk and handed me five thousand in hundred-dollar bills. "For you," he said pulling back his hand. It startled me. "Even though you did her, man." Then he handed me the money.

I pocketed the cash and walked with Lou outside into the bright sunlight, dripping sweat and swearing to each other we'd be in the shower the second we were home. The speed was wearing off so I knew I'd collapse sooner rather than later but felt an odd sense of camaraderie with Lou now that we had pulled off our plan.

But on my way home I pulled the car over. It hit me hard right there like a baseball bat that I was now an accessory after the fact. I was facing something like twenty years, even though I hadn't even done the job myself. I drove to the 109th Precinct and sat outside for a few minutes then got out and walked to the steps leading into the building. I stood there a few minutes running the story over in my head, telling them everything Lou said to me, telling them that I had slept with Rebecca, unleashing the burden Lou had just put on my back.

"Can I help you with something?" a uniformed cop asked, walking past.

I looked up without saying anything.

"You've been standing here looking at the door since I parked."

"Nothing," I said turning, and got back in my car and drove away.

* * *

SEVERAL DAYS LATER I GOT A call from my aunt that I did not expect. She was angry and yelling. "What did you bury in my shack?" she asked.

I went to see her that night and brought over some Greek food I picked up in Astoria. She adored Greek food so I brought her favorite, moussaka, and she ate it with pleasure, washing it down with some wine I also brought over. I felt odd sitting in her kitchen looking across at the shack, knowing that Rebecca was buried underneath it. My aunt oddly said nothing until she glared at me from across the table.

"Who did you bury in my shack?" she asked this time with her face in my face.

"You asked me that over the phone. What are you talking about?"

"Do be a wiseass with me. I walked around in there. I could see where you dug up the dirt. You didn't put drugs in there—you put a *body* in my backyard."

Realizing it was time to tell her the truth, I did. I explained it all. After I did she got quiet again and ate her dinner. After a few minutes she sat back and sipped her wine, placing the glass back on the table.

"I want twenty grand more," was all she said and went back to her plate.

It annoyed me my own aunt would squeeze me like this but I really had no choice. "Look, I am in this too," I told her. "You know I can't find that kind of money on my own."

"Then ask your partner," she shot back at me. "He killed this poor girl. Let him pay me to shut up. It's worth it to him. And if he doesn't pay up by the end of the week I call the cops, you got that?"

I nodded but stayed quiet. She was now backing me into a wall.

"Sorry to see you in this mess. Sorry you are bringing me into it. But maybe they'll never find her," she told me.

"Yeah, that's the plan," I said.

"They'll look for her, though. You can count on that for

sure. If she was as gorgeous as you say, a beauty like that will make the papers. What are you asking for from this Lou?"

"I didn't think of asking for anything. I slept with her behind his back," I told her.

"Men and your dicks," she told me.

"Did your neighbors hear anything?" I asked.

"Not a peep from any of them yet. But I think it's best you don't come around for a while. A year for sure. In case they look for her," she told me. "Of course, *after* you give me my money."

"You would put me on the spot?" I asked.

"You put yourself there. Don't blame me."

"Then help me out," I said.

She looked right at me. "How much did he give you? He had to give you something."

"Five grand," I reluctantly told her.

"I want some of that now to keep quiet."

"He already gave you five," I said.

"I lost big in AC."

I counted out a few thousand from the cash I had in my wallet and handed it to her.

"You can fuck yourself, Aunt. With all the money I've given you over the years? I need this," I said and walked out, shutting the door hard behind me when I left.

On my drive home it occurred to me what a hardass she was, reminding me that she walked out on her only daughter.

When I got home I called Nancy but all I got was a lot of rings so I found a card game in Bayside. I made myself a few hundred with some marginal hands and went home. My phone was ringing when I came in. I quickly picked it up. It was Aunt Leigh.

"You go fuck *yourself*," she said sounding pretty bombed from the wine. "You owe me money," she slurred. I hung up and decided to take her advice and keep my distance for a while.

I called Lou and told him what had happened with my aunt and how much money she wanted. He didn't sound too thrilled so I went over to see him. When I got there Durrico's car was parked out front. I was reluctant to walk into Lou's office but I did just the same. I found them face to face in the small office. I could see that Lou was in overalls and a blue shirt. Durrico was wearing black slacks and a bright blue silk shirt. He wore a straw fedora and sunglasses even in the office. "What did you guys do with her?" he asked.

"What you talking about?" Lou asked.

"Rebecca's gone. A few days now," he said.

"Really?" Lou said sarcastically. "She probably met some-body. Maybe a busboy at the Hilton. With a chick like that you never know."

I knew Lou was pushing it and Durrico was livid.

"Anyway, what are you asking me for? She's your girl now, not mine," Lou answered.

"Where is she, Lou?" Durrico said.

"I have no clue, Charlie."

Durrico took a closer look at Lou. "Where'd you get that scratch on your face, my friend?"

Lou glared at Durrico and closed his mouth tightly. Now that Durrico mentioned it, the scratch looked more like a cut.

"If you guys did anything to her I will make you pay," he said and turned around and left the office.

"Prick," Lou mumbled for only me to hear as he watched Charlie leave. He turned to me. "Your aunt's a cunt."

"She took the five grand you gave *me*. So we only have to give her fifteen for her to shut up," I said.

"She ain't gettin' a penny more from me," he said. I saw something flicker behind his eyes. He had other ideas on how to deal with my aunt's greed.

12

I DON'T HAVE A CLEAR MEMORY of much that happened the next few days, which eventually ran into a few weeks. Lou gave me four thousand dollars worth of coke, which I would sell at double the price. I hid the coke at home under my typewriter and sold it while playing high-stakes poker games all over Long Island.

Most of the games were set up by wise guys or wannabes. I would talk to them first to make sure it was okay to deal the coke. They would agree as long as I cut them in. I would give them ten percent and split the profits with Lou fifty-fifty since I was taking the risks.

On top of that I hit a hot streak, which put me up in cash alone around twenty-five grand. I drove my beat up Pinto onto the lot on Northern Boulevard and bought myself a black 1980 Camaro for seven thousand cash.

I thought the newfound money, car and the stash of coke would help me forget about Rebecca but it didn't. I still have no idea what possessed me to agree to Lou's plan other than fear and denial. I was afraid he'd kill me if I went to the police and I was in denial that I actually participated in the cover-up of her murder.

Every time I saw Lou I thought of Rebecca and every time he'd tell me something like, "Every time I see you I think of her." I also saw Durrico a few times at a few games but I stayed away from him. When I saw that he and I were in the same hand, I went out right away even if I knew I had him beat.

I'd sit there watching him play his hand, visualizing a black-and-white photograph of my body blasted to pieces in the hallway of my apartment on the front page of the *Post* with the caption "Poker Player Shot Dead in Mob Hit."

Neither one of us ever spoke about Rebecca when we were in a game together but we didn't have to say anything. He'd just stare at me as if he was waiting for me to break.

So, a few weeks passed and I kept busy playing poker, getting high and working on my novel when the urge hit me. I'd peck away in spurts, pushing through the pages, seemingly writing better when I was high. However, reading the pages the next morning, I'd know instantly that they weren't very good and sometimes they were just plain incoherent.

However, the story was slowly emerging. I was tracing the screwed-up and lonely life of my grandfather. Through the force of my imagination or the explicit memory I had of him, I could see his sharp nose, his big open hazel eyes and his black hair swept back with a comb. I saw his broad shoulders and his muscular arms and I could hear his baritone voice. He was emerging as a real character in my story and the plot itself, how his life came to his fateful night where he killed a Nazi sympathizer on the Brooklyn Navy Yard docks, was coming to life. Despite so many badly written pages, there was something real and tangible there.

One night around dark, my phone rang and it was Nancy. Hearing her voice made me feel like we just saw one another. It was so familiar. "You got any coke?" she asked. That was all she said.

"What happened to 'hello'?" I asked.

"You have any or what?" she asked again. She sounded strung out.

"I can get some," I told her. We agreed to meet at the park where we had first kissed, which now felt like years ago. I looked at the time. "See you in an hour," I told her.

Nancy was sitting on the bench looking irritable and antsy. The streets were dead. Nobody was out. As soon as I reached her she took the vial from me, poured a line on the back of her hand and snorted it.

"What's with you?" I asked.

"I needed a hit."

"I see that."

She calmed down. She sat back on the bench and let the wind blow through her hair. "I have some shit to deal with."

"Brian?"

"Ha! Brian?" she laughed. "I won't hear from that jerk ever again after that night."

"Then what?" I asked.

"I got let go from the school," she told me.

"They fired you?"

"Yeah, they did."

"But you were an excellent teacher. You were dedicated," I said doing a line from the back of my hand.

Nancy shrugged. "I was missing classes. I told them I was sick. I was sick, too. My stomach was bad. I was getting nosebleeds, too, right in class. Bad sinus headaches and fevers."

"That's the coke."

"No shit," she said.

"Where did you get it?"

"I was copping from this girl I saw hanging around in the park. She knew somebody who was dealing. I haven't seen her in a few days so I called you."

"You bought drugs in a park from someone you didn't know?"

"Yeah, I did. I saw her there before and wasn't sure what she was doing but I figured it out. I know her family," Nancy said.

I digested what she said but something didn't seem right. We sat in silence for a while even though both our brains were racing like shooting stars, making the night as loud and bright as Times Square.

"Whatever happened to that Rebecca chick?" she asked.

"She went to Europe," I said.

"You ever sleep with her?" she asked.

I noticed a poker tell. Nancy wasn't looking at me. She asked the questions looking away. When that happens in a game it means the player doesn't want you to see what they are thinking. It bothered me so I lied.

"I never slept with her. Why do you ask?"

"Just curious," she said.

"Do you know in *Dante's Inferno* Satan is nothing more than a slobbering monster encased in ice up to his chest?" I told her.

"He's in the Ninth Circle. That's where Dante put those who betrayed. Satan has three mouths and he chews on Brutus, Cassius and Judas for all eternity," Nancy replied.

"We both are educated assholes," I grinned.

"Tell me about it," she replied.

I looked around. "I could never betray a friend."

"Who asked you to?"

I shook my head. "No one."

I reached out and took her hand in mine.

"What are you doing?" she asked.

"Holding your hand."

She pulled her hand away. "You don't care about me. Why are you acting affectionate?"

"I care about you," I told her.

She got up and walked away from me. I got up and followed her. "Look, I didn't call in the last few days because I was in a little trouble. But it's okay now. I'm sorry."

"It wasn't a few days. It was a couple of weeks," she said.

"It was?" I asked. I couldn't remember. I paced back and forth, hoping to find an answer in the sensations from the night air, the sounds of the city pulsating in the distance and all around me.

"Look, I'm losing my apartment since I can't pay the rent anymore and I can't sleep in my car because I can't make the payments. I'm down, Danny. Really down."

"Can you go to your parents for help?"

She looked down then up again. "They want me to go into a clinic first."

"What? You're not that bad," I told her.

"I know. They're crazy," Nancy replied. "Everyone around me is acting crazy."

"Come home with me," I told her.

Nancy took me in. "Where did you go? You left me all alone," she said. Tears were rolling down her face. Her mouth opened in a grimace as if she was feeling some physical pain but I knew it wasn't from that. It was her heart I broke, the heart you can't see. The one people always talk about, not the one beating in our chests.

I pulled her close and hugged her tightly. I shook her like she was a baby, hoping the rocking back and forth would comfort her.

She fell into a deep sleep. The kind druggies fall into after not sleeping for days. I had been there a few times myself. In those sleeps you don't dream. You just hibernate, hoping not to wake up. I knew that she was overwhelmed by the terror of being strung out, the terror of her life being turned upside down. She was hysterical though perfectly calm and though at the moment unconscious I knew she was struggling with the demon in her.

We sat on the bench for a long while; I wasn't sure how long. When she eventually stirred I drove her home to her parent's house. It was late but her father answered. He let her in and she disappeared behind the closed door.

On my drive home along the dark passage of the Long Island Expressway I heard "Another Brick in the Wall" playing on the radio and I thought about how I was another brick in the wall. I was no different than any other loser. I was in debt, I had no real job, I had a girlfriend I turned into a drug addict and I buried a woman my best friend murdered.

I was another brick in the wall all right, and that wall was beginning to look more and more like a prison wall.

13

WHEN PLAYING POKER YOU HAVE TO make a leap of faith that the cards in your hand are better than the cards in the other guy's. If you play like you have the second-best hand you will always come in second, and second place is for losers.

Two things happened the next day that forced me to see that my luck was changing. Good or bad it was changing.

The first was that I called the union asking about Nancy's status. I thought maybe I could find out the actual specifics of her being fired. I knew the union didn't just fire you if you were late a few times. They were a strong union who protected their members. You'd have to commit a homicide to get fired. But she did tell me she got fired so I thought perhaps there were other circumstances she didn't share with me. I thought I could help Nancy by getting some details.

While they were looking on the computer I said to the person on the other side of the line that Nancy had put in an application at my business and I wanted to know why she had been fired from her job teaching.

The union rep on the phone said, "She wasn't fired, sir. She left her position."

"Thanks," I said and hung up.

The second thing that happened was that Lou called me to come and said he wanted me to see him at his office but when I asked why he didn't answer. So, I figured he didn't want to talk about anything on the phone.

When I got to his office he was already waiting for me outside. He nodded to his caddie and I got in beside him. He took off down Meeker Avenue and just drove through the streets of Williamsburg.

"A detective came to see me about Rebecca," he said. "He's going to be calling you."

"Why me?"

"You were my driver. You drove her around. It seems she kept a journal."

"Fuck," I said. "What else?" I knew she didn't keep a journal. She told me so. But something told me to keep what I knew secret.

"This Detective Ed Tucci got a call from her parents down in Florida that they hadn't heard from her."

I looked straight ahead. "How much does this detective know?"

"He knows I paid for her plane ticket up here and put her up. He knows she left me for Durrico. He knows she moved in with Durrico. That's where all her stuff still is."

I looked to Lou. "Does he know you met with her the last time?"

"Yeah. And I told him that we had a fight and she left. That was the last time I saw her."

"Did he buy it?"

Lou looked in his rearview mirror. "Most of it. He just can't figure why she just disappeared, meaning there's no record of her grabbing a cab in front of my place."

We drove on in silence. Driving helped Lou think. It was as if the world speeding by his windows relaxed him enough to get perspective. "Look, he knows she was in my office. He might get a warrant to check it out. I think we're fine on that. I'm going to do another cleaning job tonight. Wash it all down with alcohol and that bullshit. And even if they find something proving she was there, it doesn't mean I killed her. She was in my office several times. You need three things for a murder charge. A body, a weapon, and a motive. And yeah, they can have a motive but that's not enough to pin it on me. And they don't know where the fuck her corpse is."

"True."

"I curse the day I met her," he said.

I thought it over. I remembered something. "What about the guy she was going to see. The guy taking her to Europe?"

Lou nodded. "I told Tucci that. He pretended he didn't know anything about it. But I think he was just bluffing."

"Exactly."

"This cop is playing Mister Coy."

"What do you want me to do?"

"I want you to call him. The quicker you do the more it looks like you have nothing to do with it," Lou said.

"Okay."

"And when you see him tell him the truth. The truth is always the best lie," Lou told me. He reached into his pocket. "Here's his phone number."

The next morning I called the detective and made a plan to see him down at the 109th Precinct. The Duty Sergeant at the front desk gave me an odd look when I gave my name and he told me to go up the stairs. When I got to the second floor I faced a sign on a small revolving door that was belt high. The sign read, "Wait here for a detective." So I waited there.

An average-looking guy in a dark blue polyester jacket and white shirt and dark blue tie stepped up to me from a desk in the back. "Danny Ferraro, come in. I'm Detective Eddie Tucci," he said looking at me directly and gesturing with one had to a corner of the room.

I followed him, when he stopped and turned around. "You mind if we go in the back room?"

"No," I answered.

"It's quieter in there," he said. I thought the room we were in was already pretty quiet.

Once in the room he asked me to sit down at a small table. He closed the door behind me, took off his jacket and sat facing me. "They call you Danny?" he asked.

"They do."

"You like poker so I hear."

"I do. Like most people," I answered.

"So, where do you think she is?" he asked as if we were both old friends.

"She?"

"Rebecca. That's why we're here. We can't figure where she is," he said quickly, sounding as unfriendly as possible. "Everybody is looking for her. Me, her parents, and even Charlie Durrico. Do you know where she is?"

I felt him watching every movement I made. I wasn't sure if it was better to sit back or sit up straight. I wasn't sure which posture made me look nervous and which made me look innocent. "Is she back from Europe?"

"Was she going there?"

"She told me she was," I answered.

"Her parents never heard about that," he said.

I sensed he was lying. "Did you talk with Charlie Durrico?"

He didn't move. "She left his house on the ninth of last month to see your friend Lou. That was the last time anyone saw her," he answered. "In fact, all of her stuff is still with Charlie Durrico."

"Was her stuff packed?" I asked.

"Why?"

"Like I said. She told me she was going to Europe. When I saw her she told me she was leaving Durrico and going off to Europe with some guy. Right now, she's probably in the south of France, sunbathing topless on the Riviera."

"So, that's your take on all this, huh?" Detective Tucci asked.

I sat back. I knew I didn't kill her and I figured it was better to *act* relaxed. "I saw her a couple of days before you say she disappeared, so I am telling you that is what she told me."

"That all sounds good but why hasn't she contacted her parents if she is in Europe? If she is alive anywhere, she'd be calling them by now, don't you think?"

"Maybe. Or maybe this guy from Europe sold her into white slavery."

I could tell that Detective Tucci didn't like me coming up with scenarios.

"Amazing lady, huh? The family sent me a photo. Gorgeous."

"She was."

"Were you surprised she wanted to sleep with you?" he shot at me.

"Excuse me?"

"Hey, she slept with Lou and Charlie. Why not you? You give a girl like that enough coke she'll sleep with anybody. It must have been amazing," he said.

"What?"

"A lady like that with a guy like you."

I frowned. "Really?"

"Your friend Lou said you taught school."

"I did. High school. I took a sabbatical to write a novel," I answered.

"Like Stephen King?"

"No. Nothing like him. More literary."

"So you want to be like Shakespeare?"

"He didn't write novels."

He smirked. "I liked *The Bourne Identity.*"

Now I was moving in my chair. He was getting on my nerves.

He had one of those faces that never changed from childhood to old age. Perhaps they got fatter but that was about it. His features were blah. No mystery, no charm, no style. He had dark piercing eyes, dark receding hair that was clearly going to make him prematurely bald one day soon, and his head and neck sat on very large shoulders. I figured him to be ten years older than me and exactly my height.

"You deal cocaine, Danny?" he asked.

I frowned again not saying a word.

He now became very quiet. He put his hand in front of his face waiting for me to react. I felt I needed to do a line, feeling a slight quiver in my right eye. He noticed and I looked away.

He now leaned in. "Look, anybody who hangs with Lou Santucci and Charlie Durrico is either a tough guy like them, which I know you are not, or some kind of lackey who makes money for them. I figure you deal coke when you're not playing poker. The word around is that you are a card *hustler.* You like poker and you are good at it. You also deal some coke at the game. I catch you doing that, you're looking at five years minimum with this Rockefeller law. Nowadays, you don't need to deal weight to do some nice time. And you will get caught and you will squeal like a stuck pig because you don't want to go to Sing Sing and get your asshole plowed. So, let's save you some time in the joint. You tell me where Rebecca's corpse is and I'll make sure the DA's office cuts you some slack."

I didn't move a muscle.

"She kept a journal, Danny. I know she fucked you. I know everything from what she wrote except one thing. Where she is right now."

He made his play. He raised. And I knew he was bluffing. "I have no idea where she is right now."

Now *he* sat back.

"Do you play?" I asked.

"Poker? Sometimes."

"What, seven-card?"

"Yeah," he answered.

I looked around the table searching out the sucker and I saw that it wasn't me. "I'd like to play in a game with you. I bet you'd give away your cards every hand."

"Really? Why is that?" he asked, interested.

I was quiet. Detective Tucci did give away his hand, or that was how I saw it. He knew nothing about Rebecca's disappearance. His big play was that I was not hard and he could easily bluff me. Plus, making up that she had a journal when I knew from her own lips that she didn't keep one.

I have been bluffed before but not for big stakes like this. My life was in the pot and I knew that as long as I stayed quiet and my Aunt Leigh didn't talk and Lou kept his mouth shut, they would never find Rebecca's corpse. Unless by accident and there was nothing you could do about that kind of luck.

I knew Lou would never say a word since he was looking at life in prison. My aunt and I were accessories to the homicide so we had no reason to rat ourselves out. The homicide detective played his hand and he played it badly.

"We should play some high-stakes cash poker, Detective Tucci."

"You want me and you to play a game?" he asked.

"Actually, we just did," I said. I got up. Detective Tucci sat up. "Where you going?"

"Home."

He stood in my path and I looked at him. "You played your hand, detective. And I hope you don't mind me saying this, but you must really suck at poker."

I walked past him and out of the precinct.

* * *

THAT NIGHT I HUNG WITH NANCY and we did a few lines hanging out my window on the fire escape. I wanted to tell her all about Rebecca but I knew that was wrong. Three of us knew where she was buried and that was enough.

"You need nice clothes. I'm going to buy you some nice clothes," I told her. I knew it was the coke talking but that was okay. She was just as stoned.

"I want to go for my master's in education, Danny."

"Then let's make that happen," I told her.

"How are we going to make that happen?" she asked.

I didn't answer her but the rest of night we stayed high and I struggled to remain focused, sensing there was a "move" here, a "bet" I could make that might change my life and Nancy's.

The first thing the next morning we took the 7 subway line to midtown and I bought Nancy some fine clothes. I also bought myself a dark brown leather jacket and a gold chain.

That night, we got dressed up and went to Visage. We hung out at the bar and I bought a hundred-dollar bottle of Mumm's in honor of Rebecca without telling Nancy and we drank it slowly, doing periodic hits of coke in the bathroom.

Sometime near eleven Charlie Durrico came into Visage with a couple of goons. He sauntered right up to the bar and I offered him some of my champagne. He ignored my offer and ordered his own bottle and turned to me. "Lou must have paid you off big time," he said.

"Poker winnings, Charlie," I answered.

Durrico looked at Nancy. "You Danny's girl?"

"I am," she answered.

"Did you know your boyfriend has ice in his veins? He can be questioned by one of the best detectives in New York City and get up and walk out on him," he told her.

I was puzzled, wondering how he knew such information.

Durrico read my look. "Tucci's my cousin's asshole buddy from Arthur Avenue up in the Bronx. He told me how you stood up to him. You got balls, Danny."

Durrico leaned into me so Nancy wouldn't hear him. "I dug Rebecca. I'm not going to forget what you and your friend did."

Durrico walked away and Nancy whispered in my ear. "Why did a homicide detective want to talk to you?"

I figured I'd tell her the truth. It's always the best lie. "Do you remember that pretty girl Rebecca? The girl Lou flew up from Florida? Well, she disappeared. She went to Europe with some guy but for some reason they think she's missing and the cops are looking for her," I told her and it was the truth up to a point.

"They'll find her when she gets back," Nancy said. "But then again, she might not come back. She might marry a prince and become a princess."

As Nancy was saying this, Lou walked into the bar with a young slim pretty black girl. Lou didn't even hesitate and walked right over to me and Durrico.

Durrico glared him as Lou shook my hand and introduced his girl around to everyone. "This is Cindy."

Cindy was probably no more than twenty-one and for some reason I immediately saw the mother-of-pearl earrings. Lou had given them to *her*.

I inched over to Lou and whispered to him under the music. "Why did you give her the mother-of-pearl?"

He grabbed my arm and talked into my left ear. "It's perfect. I was in love with somebody else is what they'll think." He started gripping my arm even tighter.

"Your fuckin' aunt called me. She got the office number out of the phone book or she knows somebody who knows *of* me but we gotta talk about her pronto."

14

ONE THING ABOUT POKER IS THAT when you are on a hot streak it's best to play every hand. If you're winning everything hits. You'd hate yourself and go on tilt if you threw away an ace-high winning hand just because you didn't think it was the winner, no matter how big or how little the pot.

However, there is a problem to playing like this. The problem with being on a winning streak is that eventually it ends and it ends as quickly as it starts. You hope to know that it's over, count your winnings and quit, but nobody likes to quit. If you were a quitter you wouldn't be in the game.

Lou was strung out when I met him at his office. It was a rainy morning and he was sitting in his metal chair at his big metal desk facing a cup of coffee and a half-eaten donut. "We gotta do your aunt," he told me.

"What?"

"She can't fuckin' call me, Danny. What the fuck is that drunk bitch doing calling me here at my office? What, is she going to call me at home next? Is she going to call my wife? Is that what I have to look forward to?" Lou was furious.

"It won't happen again," I said.

"I know she's gonna break. I say we go there tonight and do her and then bury her next to Rebecca."

"I can't do that," I said.

Lou looked up at me. "You don't say 'no' to me."

I stood my ground. "My aunt is tougher than you'll ever be. She has her money and she will keep her mouth shut," I said.

Lou lowered his jaw. He scratched his head and moved forward in his chair. "This Detective Tucci called me again."

"And said what?"

Lou looked around as if he was searching for something. "Nothing new. He's probing. He said he's getting a warrant to check my place out."

"He said 'getting,' right?"

"Getting."

"He didn't say he had one?"

"Right," Lou answered.

"You said you cleaned it up in here, right?"

"I did. I spent every night in the week rubbing down everything she touched with soap and water, hydrogen peroxide, salt, spit, you name it."

"So don't worry," I said.

Lou was quiet. I knew he was still thinking about my aunt.

"My aunt is our best ally," I said.

"How's that?"

"She's in too deep, Lou. We got Rebecca there how long now? Every day that goes by my aunt is in deeper. If she talks we talk. We say she helped us bury her there in her shack. How else could we have done it without her giving us the okay?"

"She's an accessory," Lou said.

"She's looking at five to ten minimum."

"She took money. Minimum ten."

I nodded. And that ended any more talk about my aunt.

Saturday was a drizzly day but I drove the new Camaro with Nancy in it to Durrico's house and handed over the keys to the valet parking guys. There were several dozen people there including Nicky "Shoes," Joe "Duck," Eddie "The Polack" and other tough guys from Brooklyn and Queens whose faces I knew but I tried not to know their names.

Lou showed up with Cindy and stayed close to me and Nancy. Cindy tried her best to be friendly with me but I had a problem with her wearing the mother-of-pearl earrings only because I thought it was best that they were never seen again.

The music was blasting from speakers everywhere and by dark the rain let up and we were all outside on the lawn. Waitresses and waiters were everywhere with trays taking drink requests and clearly looking the other way when the guests were doing lines of coke right out in the open.

Some young lady, clearly stoned, showed up with a video camera thinking it was a good idea to tape the party but a middle-aged wise guy from Jersey I had never seen before went up to her and pulled it right out of her hands. She made a scene but nobody came to her defense, including her well-put-together boyfriend, who upon recognizing the middle-aged man as a very well-connected wise guy, turned pale and apologized to him for her behavior.

The middle-aged man accepted the apology and told the boyfriend it'd be better if he took his girlfriend and left, which they did immediately despite her protests that she didn't finish her drink.

I heard the middle-aged wise guy say as he watched them leave, "Be smart when you pick your woman. She can get you killed as fast, or even faster, than any other stupid thing you do."

It wasn't clear why Durrico threw the party. He had a slender blond on his arm, looking more like a Barbie doll than an actual human female, but she certainly made an impression and in a way I realized that was the kind of woman he actually felt comfortable with instead of someone out of his league like Rebecca. Maybe he was just interested in showing her off to everyone.

There was an expensive spread out back by the pool with shrimp, lobster tails and caviar, but no one was interested in food. They were interested in getting high.

After mingling for a bit I saw Durrico and his blond date smoking something in a round, glass-stemmed pipe under the bright florescent lights in the kitchen.

Durrico started telling everyone they were freebasing cocaine. This was when you mixed the coke with ether and siphoned it off, then, after a bit of time white crystals formed and you smoked those and you had the top of your head shot to the moon.

Durrico was sharing this new high with everyone in his part of the room and though I tried it and liked it, I was afraid for Nancy and for good reason. Later that night I found her upstairs with her top off with Durrico and his Barbie doll girlfriend freebasing in his bedroom.

"What the fuck, Nancy?" I asked.

Her eyes were ten times bigger than normal. She was so smashed I thought she didn't recognize me at first. The Barbie girl had one knee on the bed, leaning over Nancy and licking her nipples and then turning to lick her own nipples.

Durrico was standing next to them with his pants down around his knees, grinning ear to ear. "Fuckin' insane this freebasing, huh?"

I tried pulling Nancy away but she wouldn't leave the bed. Instead, she pushed *me* away and shouted to Durrico. "I want more."

"Hate to say it Danny, but you got a slut for a girlfriend," he said.

I was shattered with feelings of guilt and remorse. "Fuck it," I said turning my back on all three of them and walking out of the room.

"Revenge is sweet," Durrico shouted at me.

On my drive back to my place some things were coming into focus. "You Shook Me All Night Long" by AC/DC played on the radio. Its driving rhythm distracted me enough not to feel anything but anger for Nancy.

But then I started to think. I was thinking how she lied to me about losing her job and asked a lot of questions about Rebecca. Seeing her with Durrico the way I just had gave me more suspicions.

When I got home I took all of Nancy's things and put them in a box at the door. I sat at my window and just looked out at the night sky. Nancy didn't come home and I fell asleep when the sun came up. I only slept a few hours. Every time I woke up I thought of her and when I did I felt a tremendous amount of heartache.

That Sunday afternoon I went to Michael's restaurant and sat with him, doing all I could to eat.

"You don't want this kind of life, Danny," Michael said to me. "The world is headed in a bad direction. Get off the train and get back to teaching."

"I can't go back," I said.

"You look awful, man, and you smell like a druggie," he told me.

I was shocked but he was right. I was a druggie.

"You were a smart guy, teaching and writing, and now look at you," he said. "Lou and Charlie Durrico are lowlifes compared to you. You have to set your life on the right path, Danny. Can I help you do that?"

"I'm not like Lou or Durrico, am I?" I asked, wanting to hear that I wasn't.

"You're not. You never were. You just got caught up in it all." Michael sat back. "I still can't get over something."

"What?" I asked noticing the Sunday paper in front of him.

"How the Mafia killed the president of Sicily. This guy Mattarella was shot dead in his car with his bodyguards. *Madone*, they are nuts over there on the other side."

I picked up the newspaper. "Iranian terrorists took over the Iranian embassy in London," I said to myself.

"Yeah and the SAS killed them all. Now that's how you do it," Michael said. "Not like this bullshit we are doing. Letting them push us around. Carter sucks."

I nodded. "The Romans almost lost to Carthage in the Punic Wars. They knew how to handle a problem."

"Hannibal almost captured Rome in their last Punic War," Michael interjected.

"So some twenty years later they hunted him down and killed him, and the Roman senate decided to invade Carthage even though the country didn't have an army. They were afraid of Carthage, not then, but twenty years from then. So do you know what they did?"

"What did they do, professor?" Michael asked.

"They sent down an army to Carthage and killed every living person, sold fifty thousand survivors into slavery and put salt in all their fields so that nothing would ever grow. That way no one from Carthage could form an army and attack Rome ever again," I said.

"Smart guys those Romans."

"That is what you call a Carthaginian peace."

I thanked Michael for talking to me and when I got home Nancy was waiting there outside my building.

I went to the front door and let her in. She rushed past me. "I want my things," she said.

"You can have them. They're in a box by the door."

"Fuck you," she said.

"You moving in with your parents?"

"I'm moving in with Charlie."

"Why?"

"It's just better for me right now," she answered.

"What did I do to you?" I asked.

"I need someone really strong right now and that definitely isn't you."

"Is that why you quit your job? You think Charlie is going to take care of you?"

She was livid. "You checked up on me?"

"I called the union to find out if I could help you. I was looking to help you," I said.

Looking at her I knew it would be for the last time, at least as lovers. "You're only going with him because he gives you free drugs."

She threw at me the first thing she could pick up. It was a metal beer mug I didn't remember I owned. I ducked and it hit the door but didn't do anything but make a lot of noise.

Realizing what she had done she stopped and looked directly at me.

"I cared about you, Nancy." I looked into her soft brown eyes and her soft features, remembering when we first met how joyful she was and how innocent in her own way. Now, when I looked at her, I could see she had put up a wall. The wall didn't make her any tougher or more experienced; it just made her seem more vulnerable. She was just another brick in that wall.

I stepped away and she walked out to the elevator. I closed the door and sat in the dark the rest of the night.

* * *

THE NEXT DAY MY AUNT CALLED and told me to come right over so I drove out to her house. Once inside, she took me to the kitchen window. "The dog in the next yard knows we got something buried in the shack."

"What are you talking about?"

"He stands by the fence and barks at the shack."

"We wrapped her in plastic. He can't smell anything."

"These fucking dogs have a sixth sense. They know."

The minute I walked in I could see that my aunt had spent some of her money on new furniture, a new paint job and some very new clothing. She was also drinking a highball and it wasn't even the afternoon.

We sat at the table and I took a closer look. She had her hair done and some surgery on her face. It wasn't done very well and it made her look oddly older as if she had been a burn victim and never recovered. Her eyes were tighter and the skin under them pulled in. Her lips were swollen and her nose—which was always interesting because she had broken it when she was a little kid and it gave her pretty face character—now looked as if someone melted it on and she looked like the scarecrow in the *Wizard of Oz*.

"I want more money," she said.

I was afraid that was the entire reason she called me. "From who?"

"From this Lou friend of yours," she answered.

"Aunt, we made a deal and now you want to renege? Do you know who you are dealing with?"

She sipped her highball. "I told you I wanted more. Where is it?"

"Didn't you put the money away like you said you were going to do?"

"I put some in the house, I put some into my health and I lost some down in AC."

"Fuck," I said.

I got up. I walked to the window. "I'd rather kill the dog than see Lou bury you in there with her." I turned back to her.

Aunt Leigh didn't move. She was as hard as they come. "Let me see him try."

"You are trying to extort more cash from him. He will do just that if I ask for more."

"I don't care."

"What's the reason I tell him that you want more cash?"

"I need it, tell him. He doesn't have to know why I want it. I hold the cards, nephew," she told me and threw her drink back and made another.

I knew I had a problem and what was worse was that my aunt wasn't stupid. I had to learn why she was acting this way. "You want this money so badly you would screw this whole thing up over it?" I asked.

She sat at the table and glared at me. "I know you're both laughing behind my back. You think you can take advantage of me because I'm a woman."

Maybe that was it? "Nobody takes advantage of you," I told her to try and calm her down.

I got close and looked her straight in the eyes. "We can't move her. We can't do anything now. What it *is*, is what it is. There's a detective asking questions. He's at a dead end and you know why? Lou won't say shit because he killed her. I won't say anything because I'm involved in covering up the murder and so are you. Rebecca's remains are only a few yards away from both of us but we're golden because we are the only people who know this fact. So as long as you and I keep quiet we'll all get away with this. *We* hold the cards, Aunt Leigh."

"Can you get more money out of him?" she asked.

"You're thinking crazy," I told her.

She got up and walked to the door. "I'll sell this house and when they find the girl, I'll be long gone and you and your friend will be doing time."

I took a deep breath and walked outside into the backyard. My aunt kept the backyard dark but I managed to walk to the shack. I heard the dog in the next yard scamper over to the fence. The dog didn't bark at first but I saw the next-door neighbor's backyard light flash on. The dog was silhouetted in the light and I was now standing in front of the shack. I couldn't smell a thing. I tried the door and it was locked. The dog barked twice and then was quiet.

My aunt left the house and walked up to me. She was standing in the light so I could make out her face.

"I don't smell anything," I said quietly.

"You callin' me a liar?" she asked.

Before I could answer she smacked me across the face. The smack was so loud the dog barked.

My aunt was smaller than me even in her lifts. When she smacked me, she reached up and caught me right below my ear on my cheek.

I felt the sting and a surge of anger reach up from my stomach to my brain. Her eyes were on fire in the light and I could see she was drunk. I don't know what possessed me but I was so frustrated. I was about to hit her when I stopped myself, grabbed her by her long black hair, and tugged it so hard, she let out a yelp. I dragged her through the backyard and back into the house, closing the door behind us.

She struggled with me, biting, trying to rip out my eyes, clawing at my hands and trying to kick me and though drunk, she was still alert enough to know not to make any noise that would attract the neighbors.

Once I got her into the house I slammed shut the kitchen the door and shoved her across the room.

"What the fuck is wrong with you?" I shouted.

She fell forward, knocking into the table. She grabbed her empty bottle of booze and swung it at me, grazing me right above my right eye. However, I managed to dodge the full-on assault of her attack.

My aunt was a petite woman and the full force of her swing took her off her feet and she went flying by me. She lost her balance and without me lifting an arm against her, she managed to crash headlong into her refrigerator.

I heard the crack of her head hitting the refrigerator door and saw blood trickle across the light blue door. She crumpled, sliding down to the kitchen floor and moaning.

"Fuck," I said looking down at her at my feet. She was lying on her back holding her head, with a large bruise right above her eye.

"Aunt, *what* the fuck?" I said to her.

"It hurts," she told me.

I bent down to lift her up but as I did, she grabbed my right cheek and dug her fingernails deep into my flesh.

Now it was my time to moan as she screamed with a drunk, psychotic and manic growl that came from her bowels. It horrified me so much I lost all control and punched her right in the center of her jaw so hard I felt the pain shoot up my own fist to my chin but it worked and it knocked her out.

I got up and stood over her.

I placed my unconscious aunt on the bed and I put a large icepack on the bump on her forehead that she had put there herself and I placed a smaller icepack on her jaw from the bruise I had put there.

When she woke up both her eyes were swollen and she stared at me for a few seconds.

"Do you remember what happened?" I asked.

She nodded. "My head is killing me."

"I'm fucking lucky you didn't kill me," I told her pointing to the slight bump on my forehead from the bottle and the deep red lines on my arm from her nails.

"Put peroxide on that," she said, her voice barely audible.

"Thanks," I told her. I was still angry not only at her stupid behavior but also at her desire to extort more money from Lou.

I also felt this weird sense of intimacy I just had with my aunt, more bizarre than even when she molested me all those years ago. Now she was a middle-aged woman and we were physically hitting one another as if we were sworn and violent enemies. In some odd way now that the fighting was over I felt closer to her, though in no way did that diminish my concern for her sanity and the danger she was putting us in.

"I'm going home and I don't want to hear anymore talk about money. Do you hear me?" I asked.

She was quiet and I could see the look of an insane person when I looked deep into her eyes. My Aunt Leigh was no different than any other psychopath who lacked a conscience.

She didn't answer me and I didn't care. I knew she got the message. I was her nephew but I was protecting myself and if she did anything crazy again, like talking about calling the police, I would wash my hands of her and leave her to Lou.

"I will leave you to Lou if you do this again," I said making sure she didn't need to read my mind.

When I walked out of the house I went halfway across the backyard again, stopped and stood in the dark looking at the shack. It was eerie knowing Rebecca's remains were quietly in repose only a few yards away in the dark and a powerful threat to my future.

15

THE NEXT NIGHT WITH COKE AND cash in my pockets I went to Visage and ordered my own bottle of Moët. I needed to go out and be among the living, hoping to forget my situation. I sat alone at the bar on the second floor flirting with the sexy bartender who I poured an extra glass for. She told me the boss was out for the night and she'd be happy to take a sip. It was a weeknight and the club wasn't very crowded.

After only a few glasses of champagne I noticed a couple to my left. He was my height and around my age with thin blond hair and glasses. His hair was neatly cut and combed back and he wore a beige suit. She was the same height with long red hair and had a "smart" look about her, dressed in a dark business suit.

I overheard the word "editor" and it got my full attention. In a few minutes I introduced myself and offered them a glass of Moët. He resisted but she didn't and I soon found out that they were junior editors at Simon & Schuster Publishing House and were in the fiction department. His name was Bennett Williams and she was Chloe Smith and they were out celebrating an author getting a rave review in *Publisher's Weekly* and *Library Journal.*

We got into an interesting conversation about the publishing world along with Visage and champagne, which Chloe enjoyed but Bennett didn't as much. I called him Will. The name William took too long to say and I felt like I was back in grammar school every time I said it.

"You like coke?" I asked them both but neither answered.

I pulled a vial from my pocket and nodded to the restrooms. "Go do a hit."

Bennett looked agitated while Chloe smiled. "I have an important meeting tomorrow morning," she said. "If this were a Friday night, I'd be all for it," she told me and kissed Bennett on the cheek and handed me her card discreetly enough that it made me think she didn't want him to see what she was doing and left.

"She's very sharp," Bennett said as she walked away.

"Nice. You guys involved?" I asked.

"Oh, no. We just work together." Seeing that he was now alone, Bennett asked me for the vial. "I wouldn't mind if the offer still stands."

"Sure," I told him and handed him the vial.

Bennett took the vial and went into the bathroom. Minutes later he was back and I could see the whites of his pale blue eyes looked brighter than they did before he did the coke.

We were taking turns doing hits, sitting back at the bar and talking publishing and writing, which led me to tell him about my novel-in-progress.

When I mentioned how my grandfather had some "dealings" with the Mafia in the neighborhood, Bennett, who was from Westport, Connecticut, and looked like he stepped out of a Bloomingdale's ad, was enthralled. He wanted to hear all the stories I had been living, including the night in the Waldorf, the illegal poker games and soon it became an amazing night for me because I was able to talk through my story about my grandfather, throwing in actual events from my own life and figuring out how to pull it off in literary terms. I was doing all this with a professional editor. If I had walked into the offices of Simon & Schuster with my manuscript I wouldn't have gotten any attention. The great irony was that it was all being done in Visage with champagne and cocaine and I was the center of attention.

We were talking a mile a minute, sharing ideas and expressing our views on contemporary fiction, which I used to read back in my college days, and sounding like identical twins all thanks to the coke.

I found out that we even shared a love of *Loon Lake* and I told him how much I wanted my novel to be like that one even though I was really stretching it but who cared? The coke made me feel like a genius.

Despite my being high I saw Bennett for what he was: a rich guy fascinated with the underworld and bad boys and their women. Bennett was clearly juiced by the danger and feeling more like a man than he probably felt in his office where he kissed ass every day and put red lines through manuscripts.

Somewhere near two in the morning we left Visage and went to Sarge's Diner on the East Side and ordered ham and eggs. I told him about the gorgeous women that hung around the champagne and cocaine. I was tempting Bennett, knowing that he would love to get close to a woman like Rebecca, daydreaming of taking them on his family yacht and getting a blow job down below after cocktails and watching his

Rebecca-like woman walk around in her bikini until tossing off her top just for him.

Eventually, I drove Bennett to his apartment on East Ninety-First and as I was dropping him off I heard the words I was waiting to hear. "I'd love to read what you wrote, Danny, send it to me."

"How about we hang this weekend and I'll get a couple of women to party with us?" I said.

Bennett hesitated. I wasn't sure why. He grinned, shook my hand and got out of the car.

I spent the next four days writing a hundred pages, only breaking up the writing with poker games where I was playing it coy and conservative, keeping my bluffing to a minimum and only staying in the pot when I had a strong hand, assuring me that I'd be going home with more cash than I started with or breaking even.

A week later I made a copy of my first hundred pages of my untitled novel using all the notes I had taken down in my head and applying them to what I had already written. The novel was taking real shape, flashing back and forth to my grandfather's life working as a security guard at the Brooklyn Navy Yard during World War II and my life struggling to complete my novel and pay the rent by dealing cocaine and playing high stakes poker.

I left a copy of the novel at the front desk at Simon & Shuster and a short note for Bennett Williams with my phone number. Now I had to wait.

* * *

I PLAYED POKER ALL THAT WEEK and found myself in games with bad players. The kind of players I liked were those who were aggressive but reckless. I liked to trap them. It takes time but I had a lot of that. Patience is the best ingredient to lay a trap and I'd wait a few hours into the game before I sprang my best ones. I'd wait until I was in a good position to call a bluff, or just not raise when I had a monster hand and instead check raise or three bet.

Sometimes that works for you but other times you can be too coy and the entire hand can explode in your face when you give the other guy a chance to catch a card.

I made a few thousand the next few nights playing tight, then called Lou to see if we could take Bennett out on Lou's cabin cruiser since weather was getting warmer. Lou had the boat docked on the south shore and liked to take it out on a Saturday when he had a lady to impress. He would usually wait until his wife was away for the weekend, then he'd give me a call that he was going out. I was one of his few friends who was still single and could follow him at the drop of a hat.

I was in luck when I called. Lou was about to call me. He was taking the boat out with Cindy and she was bringing a friend. I asked him if I could bring two people and he said it was okay and told me to meet him at a dock in Long Beach at ten a.m.

I immediately called Bennett and invited him on the boat and to ask Chloe to come along. He said he was definitely up for a day on the boat. I told him that he and Chloe could meet me at the Broadway stop on the Port Washington line on the Long Island Railroad if they left Penn Station right before nine.

He didn't say anything about my manuscript so I thought it best not to bring it up. I should wait until we were on the boat or even better I should wait until he brought it up.

Bennett and Chloe got off the train at the Broadway stop and I had to smile to myself as they walked to me. Bennett was wearing white shorts, a bright blue plaid shirt and sandals. Chloe wore a long white summer dress and sandals. She had her long red hair pulled back in a loose white and black scarf and her skin was pale, even paler to me than when I first saw her in Visage. She wore bright red nail polish, which was enhanced by the bright sunlight. With both dressed the way they were, wearing sunglasses and carrying their things in overnight bags, they certainly didn't fit in with the black T-shirt, gold jewelry-wearing crowd.

I was in jeans and sneakers with a black T-shirt. I was barely awake. I usually slept till noon so now I was functioning at about four hours of sleep tops.

As soon as they got into the car with Bennett in the back and Chloe in the front, I quickly drove east on the Long Island Expressway.

Lou and Cindy and her girlfriend Nell were waiting for us when we arrived. Nell was goofy, white and vivacious, wearing a long light gray-and-blue summer smock, which was meant to hide her sleek figure. She had a big smile and flowing brown hair and giggled at everything anyone said. I could see how both Cindy and Nell had to be strippers, just by the way they were so comfortable and confident in the way they carried their bodies when they walked and moved. I also knew from dating some in the past how they starved themselves and if you invited them out for pizza they'd jump. They suffered from lack of finances and the knowledge that if they gained weight they'd lose work.

I quickly introduced Lou, Cindy and Nell to Bennett and Chloe and in minutes we were pushing away from the dock and a few minutes after that we flying over the blue waters of the Great South Bay.

Lou was a good and responsible boat captain, standing behind the boat's wheel, having Cindy show us where all the life preservers were stored and how we should stay in our seats starboard when we were moving through the bay.

The sky and bay blended at the horizon and everywhere I looked was blue and despite my lack of sleep I was thrilled to be out in the air, sea and sky on the thirty-five-foot cruiser, mostly because Bennett had read my manuscript.

We spent most of the trip just smiling at one another since serious conversation was nearly impossible with the engine roaring beneath us.

Lou took the cruiser east and eventually he lowered the anchor and "parked" the boat in sight of the shore. As soon as we did, Lou blasted his stereo and "Funkytown" annihilated the silence on the bay, making even the seagulls take flight.

"That's Fire Island," he told us opening up his icebox and revealing several bottles of champagne.

"I like Mumm's," Cindy said.

I smiled.

"Lou told me to say that," Cindy said.

I smiled again.

Cindy got some plastic cups and we all toasted Lou on his boat, his invitation and our luck in having a gorgeous day.

I barely tasted the champagne and sat with Bennett and Chloe, making sure they were comfortable. Lou was a terrific host, bringing Nell and Cindy into our conversation.

"So, you two are publishers?" he asked.

"Editors," Bennett answered.

"Same shit, no?" Lou said.

I smiled and chimed in. "Bennett is reading my manuscript. The novel I am working on about my grandfather."

"Oh, it's much more than that," Chloe stated. "Or so I heard."

"Oh yeah, what's it about?" Lou asked suspiciously.

I frowned. "It's about you, Lou."

"No, shit?"

I could see Lou getting worried.

"I'm kidding. It's about my grandfather's life and my life and how we are both so different," I said.

That seemed to placate Lou and he went back to pouring champagne and brought Cindy up to the bow. Bennett, Chloe, Nell and I sat starboard out of the sun, which was blocked by the canopy roof.

"I love reading," Nell blurted out.

"What do you read?" Chloe asked.

"Romance novels mostly. Harlequin," she answered.

"Our strongest competition," Chloe replied.

"What do you do?" Bennett asked.

"I dance. At clubs. You know, high-end dance clubs," she answered. She and Chloe started talking intensely about how much money Nell made and how different the hours were between dancing nights for money and editing novels during the day. I was happy to see Chloe was open to Nell's lifestyle.

It gave me time to maneuver the conversation with Bennett around to my manuscript. "You get through it yet?" I asked.

I could see that Bennett was more enthralled with Nell than me. He sat across from her eyeing her tanned shoulders.

"Read it. Like it a lot," he answered.

"Great," I said.

"You do any more work on it?" he asked.

"Not much. I wanted your reaction first to see if you had any notes for me," I answered.

Bennett was antsy. I could see that he wanted to get into a conversation with Nell.

"What club do you dance in, may I ask?" Chloe asked.

"Hustler mostly and Billy's Topless downtown. They have a good happy hour, actually. It's a dive but really cool. Kind of like a neighborhood biker bar. You two should both come by one night," Nell said with the invite directed more to Chloe than Bennett.

Bennett was unfazed and Chloe seemed enchanted but I was persistent. "Do you have any notes?"

Bennett looked at me as if he had no idea what I was talking about.

"For my book?"

He nodded. "Oh, yes. I just wanted to roll them around in my head. I'll send them to you first thing Monday morning."

Chloe smiled at me. She was smart enough to get what was happening or, in my mind, she was privy to some information I was not aware of.

I saw Lou walking along the boat portside and he gestured at me to come down into the cabin. I got up and followed him.

Once down in the cabin, he put a line of coke on the table and did a hit. "I'm not getting your friends high," he said.

"It's okay. I brought some along."

"They are weird. What's the deal? This guy likes your book?"

"I hope he does."

"Watch out he doesn't play you," Lou told me.

I appreciated the insight. "You think that's his story?"

"Yeah, when does a schmuck like that get to have broads like we got on the boat with us now? Cindy and Nell are top dollar. Nell is from somewhere up near Albany. She moved into the city. I figured you'd dig her and she'd dig you. His girl ain't bad but still."

"She's not with him like that. She's a friend. I asked her along to make him comfortable."

"She's a dyke," Lou shot back.

"Really? You think?" I asked.

"She's non-stop talking to Nell, and even Cindy, who loves everybody, told me that Nell said to her that this Chloe hasn't taken her eyes off of her tits and ass since we left the dock," Lou said.

"I like Nell," I said. "She's hot. But I think he likes her."

"Look, pal, do what you have to do."

I nodded.

"How's the aunt?" he asked.

I felt my heart in my throat. "She's nuts but she's cool."

Lou got quiet.

"She's cool." I thought of how I left her back at her house with the lumps on her head and jaw and when I looked back at Lou I smiled, glad I never gave either one of them the other's phone number.

"To tell you the truth, I gave her a beating," I said. "She won't be a problem."

"Good for you," Lou said.

Once topside, we all made our way to the bow with the community decision of getting some sun. I led the way with Chloe, Nell and Bennett following. We put some towels on the deck and sat back with our glasses of champagne.

The boat was rocking a little and the wind picked up but we held onto the lines along the port side and all managed to get to what Lou liked to call "the sun deck."

The sun was hot and the day got a lot hotter when Cindy and Nell removed their tops. Nell smiled at me when she did and I looked to Bennett who was literally sweating. They removed their tops so casually it was as if they were at work in the dark on stage.

"Like the south of France," Bennett stated.

"Fuck the south of France. This is better. I love America," Lou said out loud.

Bennett shouted back in agreement, clearly intimidated. "I just meant that you can go topless in Nice and Saint-Tropez."

I turned to Chloe and smiled at her. "Your turn."

I thought Chloe would refuse but she gave everyone a big smile in return. "I've never done this before."

"Go for it. You're among friends," Lou said lying back as Cindy covered him in suntan lotion.

Bennett now lay and looked into the sun with his black sunglasses. "Chloe is from West Palm Beach. She's always topless. Come on, Chloe, don't be coy."

Chloe laughed and removed her top. She had nearly perfectly formed, larger-than-average very pale breasts.

"Be careful you don't burn," Cindy said.

Chloe then sat back on her towel with her large straw sun hat and giggled. "I'll put suntan lotion on them."

Nell handed her the suntan lotion and Chloe took it and smothered herself with it.

"It's not fair. You guys get a free show and you have your tops off and who cares?" Cindy smiled.

"I provide the boat you provide the tits. Nothing is free in this world, baby doll," Lou stated.

I watched as Bennett now turned his body away from me and faced Nell, who was on her back and topless.

"Keep an eye out for the patrol boats," Lou said to me as I stood up and walked to the cabin's glass windows and leaned back. The boat continued rocking gently and I felt the sun beating down on my face and shoulders as I watched Bennett and wondered if Lou was right. Who was playing *who*?

While on his side and leaning on his elbow, Bennett crossed his legs and I could see his toes doing a dance as he spoke to Nell. Nell didn't look at him and though I couldn't hear the conversation I got the feeling that he was probably selling himself by casually telling her about his family yacht and house on the Sound and his membership to the Yale Club and all the things a wild and pretty young lady like Nell new to New York City fantasized about when she thought of the guy she'd like to hook up with.

"You sound like one of those guys I meet at the club," Nell shouted with a chuckle and Bennett looked embarrassed.

"I have to see you dance," he said.

Nell handed him the lotion. "Can you get my back?" she asked.

Nell turned around and was now on her stomach. Her bikini barely hid her bottom, with ass cheeks peeking out. She had lovely dusky skin and Bennett reached over and I could see that he could barely breathe as he squirted the white lotion on her back and gently rubbed it in.

I looked across the deck and on the far left was Bennett lying beside Nell who was lying beside Chloe. Lou and Cindy were down further on the bow lying side by side.

I decided to go back to the cabin and nap, which I did for a couple of hours.

In one dream I had, Rebecca was breaking through the surface of the bay and was treading water beside the boat. I looked at her but she didn't smile. Her eyes were wide open but I could tell she was still dead.

16

When I woke up, Bette Midler's "The Rose" was playing on the radio. I found the sink, washed my face, and looked out the porthole and saw that sun was still up in the sky but not as intense.

I felt as if leaden weights had been attached to my shoulders and legs. Though rested, I still felt beat up and drained. I was also starving.

I was still in my jeans and black T-shirt and Lou loved running the AC so where I had fallen asleep in the cabin was cool. When I opened the door, I could feel the wave of heat hit me and I saw everyone now starboard laughing and drinking the champagne and doing lines of coke from Lou's small gold spoon. There were also some store-bought sandwiches on the table. Most were still wrapped, so I grabbed a couple, eating ham and cheese and a chicken cutlet.

I found a can of ginger ale and drank it quickly. I saw that Cindy was wrapped around Lou as she sat on his lap. Bennett was sitting close to Nell, and Chloe was sitting with her back to everyone, facing the bay. The ladies had their tops back on and everyone looked stoned and happy. While I was asleep Lou brought out some pot for everyone. Chloe handed me a joint and I took a hit.

We all went back on the deck again to watch the sun slowly sink in the west. Lou cuddled up with Cindy while Bennett and Nell eased close to one another. Chloe sat by herself drinking champagne so I sat down next to her.

"It's gorgeous out here. What does your friend do?" she asked.

"He runs a construction business," I answered.

"I know I shouldn't ask but is he with the Mafia?" she asked.

I took her in, analyzing the difference between Chloe and the other ladies on the boat. Chloe was working hard to be comfortable with her sexuality while Cindy and Nell were just sexy without trying. Chloe was attractive but she was self-conscious about herself in ways that were hard to pin down.

"Lou is his language," I said out of nowhere.

"I get that," Chloe said, smartly reading my mind.

"Do you hear Mafia in his voice?" I asked.

"Maybe," she said.

"Then draw your own conclusions," I said playing with her though I doubt she had any notion I was.

"Cindy and Nell have little confidence in their language so they let their bodies speak for them," I said.

Chloe nodded. "And me?"

I leaned in and kissed her. She was clearly surprised but she didn't resist. I felt her tongue. Her mouth and lips were wet. I leaned back and saw she was leaning forward awkwardly in her chair.

"That was unfair. I'm a little drunk," she said.

"Do you want me to take it back?"

"No," she smiled. "I think you're a sexy man."

I didn't respond. I felt her eyes on me. They were slightly green but then everyone's eyes look that color when they are on the water.

"Bennett says you have talent. I'd like to read your pages."

"I'd like you to read them."

"I will ask him, but remember, I'm an editor for mysteries. Bennett handles the literary fiction."

"Sure, but I'd love for your reaction to my pages," I told her and kissed her again. When I stopped I said, "My next book will be a mystery."

Soon after, Lou took Cindy into his cabin where he had a full bedroom and Bennett and Nell placed a large rubber float on the ground and lay down on it. Chloe felt out of place so we grabbed a blanket and went back to the deck.

The wind picked up as the sun set so we were getting colder and huddled together under the blanket. Though I don't think either one of us was that attracted to the other we found ourselves in the awkward position of being the odd couple out so we went with the flow.

We kissed intensely but when I placed my hand on her breasts she demurred. "I don't know you well enough," she said so I stopped and we just lay back and with the blanket over us we stared up into the sky. The crescent moon floated up out of the sea and soon the blue sky turned dark blue and eventually it became black dotted with a thousand stars.

Chloe asked me if I had a girlfriend and I told her about Nancy and how I lost her to Durrico. I also told her about Rebecca being Durrico's girlfriend.

"My God, what a life you lead," she said. "No wonder you write."

I drove Bennett back to his place with Nell first and then Chloe to her apartment on East Fifty-Fourth Street. "Thanks for inviting me. I had a great time," she said kissing me on the cheek as she got out.

I sat in the car for a long moment, thinking perhaps I had actually made a new path for myself, meeting people who lived in the world I wanted to inhabit, where literature was the name of the game and not drugs and poker.

I went home refreshed from the nap I had on the boat and wrote another chapter. I spent as much time that week on the novel as I had ever. I knew I needed to play more poker to pay the rent but I did have some cash put away. I stopped dealing the coke at the games, worried about the heat from Detective Tucci and waited for Bennett to send me his notes.

* * *

A WEEK PASSED AND I DIDN'T hear a word from Bennett but I did learn from Lou that Bennett and Nell were now a regular thing. When I was given that news I called Bennett again and another few days went by without hearing back. I called Chloe at her office but she never got back to me either.

I asked Lou to set up a double date with Cindy and Nell and Bennett without telling anyone that I was going to make an appearance. Lou was all for it and picked Visage. Nell got back to Lou, telling him that Bennett wasn't that wild about going to Visage, but Lou told Nell he insisted. The night before I had dinner with Lou and Cindy at Michael's and learned a lot about Bennett and Nell.

"Bennett buys her clothes. He gives her some money for rent and takes her shopping for food. He goes to see her dance and goes home. When she gets off she takes a cab to his apartment and wakes him up and they fool around," Cindy told us digging into her spaghetti.

When the night came and they were all at Visage I waited an hour, giving everyone time to get high before I showed up. I sauntered into the VIP section on the second floor, nodded to the bouncer who recognized me and immediately walked over to the small round table where everyone was sitting.

The waitress quickly found me a fifth chair and I sat down next to Bennett having directed her to place it there.

"Hey," I said and I could see him squirm. He was clearly coked up and not happy to see me.

"Hey, Danny! I owe you a call," he said.

"You owe me a few calls but who's counting?" I said.

Bennett nodded and was sullen. "I have your notes."

"With you?" I asked.

He shook his head. I felt Lou watching me. Cindy played it cool, sitting back in her chair as Nell sipped her champagne pretending to be oblivious to the fact that she had set Bennett up.

"Let's to go the restroom," I said to him.

"But I don't have to go," he said.

I stood up. "Oh, yeah, you have to go."

"I gotta go, too," Lou said.

We waited as Bennett, his eyes darting back and forth from Nell to me, got up and walked around the corner to the bathroom as Michael Jackson played overhead.

Lou gestured to Cindy. "Order another bottle of Moët. This one's on Bennie here."

Once in the bathroom the music got louder, though it sounded odd like it always did in the men's room, as if the bass had been cut out of it.

"I really don't have to go," Bennett said to us as I noticed a guy getting out of the stall with white powder on his lip.

"You got coke on your lip, pal," Lou told him.

The guy looked in the mirror and said to Lou, "Thanks."

Lou stood with his back to the door after the guy walked out as I inched up to Bennett. "What are you playing me for?"

He shrugged. "What?"

"You're fucking one of our ladies and you don't return my call?" I said.

He arched his eyebrows and took a deep breath.

"I have more of the manuscript for you," I told him.

"Oh, good. I'll read it first thing."

"It's in the car," I said.

"Great," he answered.

Lou stepped up from behind him and smacked Bennett hard against his head right under his ear with his fist clenched halfway between a smack and a punch. Bennett moaned and buckled forward.

It was interesting watching Lou hit Bennett. Lou enjoyed it. I could see him anticipate it as if he was waiting all night, sharing jokes and drinks with Bennett but in the end just happy to have someone to physically hit.

"Don't fuck with me, Bennett."

"I won't," he managed to say.

I was struggling with several thoughts. I knew I couldn't really lose my temper because if I really told him how angry I was he'd never publish my novel; on the other hand I knew there was a chance he would never publish it anyway and was just using me. It was now my time to take a deep breath.

I fixed my stare on Bennett's Adam's apple. "I want you to be my editor."

"He's got talent, right?" Lou shot in.

"Yes," Bennett answered.

"And Nell, she's got talent, right? *Madone*, she has talent," Lou said.

Bennett had no idea how he was supposed to respond so he kept quiet.

Lou now shoved Bennett up against the wall. "You take care of my friends. Nell and Danny. You can fuck one but you can't fuck the both of them. You got that?"

Bennett was more baffled now than he was before so he just nodded.

"I'm throwing Danny a book party when it's ready," Lou said. "It's not ready yet, right Danny?"

"Not yet," I said deadpan.

Then Bennett did something odd: he reached out and touched the collar of my sports jacket as he was trying to catch his breath.

"Let's go have some fun," Lou said and left the room. I felt myself stuck to Bennett, facing him silently.

"I'm in over my head here," he told me.

"You're with friends," I said and left him.

Bennett came back to the table and Nell gave me a slight smile even though she could see how red his face was from the smack Lou gave him.

Not long after I drove Bennett and Nell back to his apartment, handing him the manuscript with more pages.

He called the next afternoon with notes on my book without mentioning the incident in the bathroom at Visage. I quickly went to work typing in all the changes he suggested and left the new manuscript with his doorman at the end of the week.

I had half the novel completed and was feeling hopeful.

17

THE WEEK MOVED QUICKLY AND THE air got hot and I did hear from Bennett. He sent me several pages of typed notes by mail. I thought they were thoughtful and helpful so I focused on making the changes and pushed on doing all I could to complete a first draft.

As I worked on my novel, Bennett continued to see Nell and I spent a lot of my nights at Michael's, having dinner and hanging out with him. Some nights it was a little depressing since he closed up around eleven and wanted to go home to his wife and all I could do at that time was go home and sit in front of the television thinking of the time when Nancy was staying with me.

Lou was still seeing Cindy during that time and, in fact, he spent more time with her than he had with any other "girl-friend" other than Rebecca. I think it was because she was so pleasant and never demanded anything from him and, most importantly, it got him out of his house. I also think he was doing it to get Rebecca out of his mind. There were more than a few times I wondered if he spoke about Rebecca to

Cindy and I hoped that he hadn't. Every man has a soft spot somewhere and most men need to share their losses with someone—even men like Lou. I found tough guys like him to be somewhat more sentimental than most others.

Those few weeks in early summer everything seemed good. I stopped hearing from my Aunt Leigh, Detective Tucci seemed to have disappeared and even Durrico seemed to have dropped off the face of the planet. I thought of Nancy a lot but now this obsession with the novel took over my life.

* * *

"MY BOSS, MR. CLARKE, READ YOUR manuscript," Bennett told me over the phone a month later. "He'd like to set up a meeting."

"Great. When?" I asked.

Bennett made an appointment for me the following Monday. I spent the entire weekend writing and only going out Sunday night with Lou and Cindy to an East Side bar.

It was there Lou and Cindy told me that Nell was pregnant with Bennett's kid. I couldn't and didn't want to believe it.

"He's gotta do the right thing here," Lou said.

"That fast? It happened that fast? What, she trapped him maybe?" I said.

"Nell's got nothing and nobody," Cindy chimed in. "She's broke. He's giving her money for her rent right now. She figures he loves her."

"Does he know about the baby?" I asked.

"She's telling him tonight," Lou answered.

The rest of the night I was on pins and needles. When my phone rang early Monday morning I wasn't surprised.

It was Bennett. "Mister Clarke has to cancel the meeting."

"Why?"

"He's not sure when we can reschedule. I'll tell you when I get a date," he told me and hung up.

I headed to the city and waited for Bennett outside his apartment that night. When he saw me there was fear in his eyes.

"We are talking now," I said walking right up to him before he could even get his key out.

"Upstairs," I said.

"No, someplace public. I don't trust you," he said.

We found an Irish pub around the corner.

I told him that I knew about Nell and he looked white as a ghost. "I'll pay for the abortion."

"She might not want one."

He looked into his beer. "I'm sick."

"You fooled around and you got caught. You have to do the right thing here," I said.

He looked at me. "What's the right thing?"

"Marry her."

"I don't love her."

"Then give her a shitload of money," I told him.

He sat back. "What's Lou going to do to me?" he asked.

"Nothing, if you do the right thing."

He looked around as if searching for something else. "I have to give up your book," he said turning to me.

"Why?"

"I have to leave New York," he said.

"So why give up the book?" I asked.

"I have to leave Simon & Schuster. I'm going to call my father and see if he can get me some work up in Stamford," he answered.

I reached across the table and grabbed his shirt right above his heart. "You fuck! You can't leave me hanging like this," I shouted.

I looked around the bar and realized everyone was looking. I eased back and watched him tremble in his chair.

"I have been working on my novel day and night."

"I don't care," he told me.

"Excuse me?"

"You did this to me," he said.

"What the fuck?"

"Chloe said you were trouble. I should have listened to her," he told me, not moving. He was waiting for me to move.

"I want to see your boss Clarke," I said.

"He won't see you."

"Did he read my manuscript?"

Bennett nodded.

"Did he like it?"

"He liked it because I liked it. That's his job. To make junior editors like me take chances. If the books we like fail, then we look bad. If he likes it too much and it fails, he looks bad. If it does well he looks even better than we do. That's how the publishing world works," he told me. "That's how any corporation works, actually."

I sat back. "You listen to me and you listen good. If you don't set up a meeting for me with your boss I will tell Lou that he should hire some goons to kick the living shit out of you. And you won't know when it will happen, pal. It can be tomorrow or next year. You will be in a bar having a great time or walking home late from a meeting. It will look like a mugging or a hit-and-run but one thing is for sure, you will have broken bones and worse," I told him knowing that I was overreacting but I had to.

"I'll tell the police," he said.

I kicked him sharply under the table, jamming my right boot into his shin. He whelped in pain. I looked around the room and smiled.

Bennett wanted no part of me. I could see it in his eyes.

"If I do that, will you tell Lou to leave me alone about Nell?"

I eyed him again. I could see that he was playing the only cards he had: the cards of mercy.

"If you give her money you are free and clear. And if you set up one meeting, one real meeting with this Mr. Clarke you can go to Stamford or wherever you can hide and all this will become a long-forgotten nightmare," I answered.

Bennett quickly got up and left. The next day he met Nell and promised her five thousand dollars in cash but on one condition: she had to have an abortion. Nell reluctantly agreed. Bennett's family attorney called Nell with a contract stating the money would be sent to her in a cashier's check once she had documentation of the abortion.

Nell had the abortion and took the money.

A few days later Bennett called me with Mister Clarke's personal assistant's phone number and I called to set up a meeting with him about my novel the following week.

* * *

IT TOOK MORE THAN A FEW weeks for Mr. Clarke to meet with me but eventually he did. While I was waiting for the meeting time passed and Nell went back to live with her family, burnt out by her short time in New York City. I didn't see her before she went.

Bennett moved out of New York and left Simon & Schuster like he said but he didn't leave a forwarding address. Even Chloe left her job and moved to Michigan to teach at some college and Lou broke up with Cindy. She was devastated and actually even called me, asking me to speak to Lou for her.

"I know he's a tough guy and he's married but I love him," Cindy told me.

I heard her out patiently and called Lou. "Cindy called me. She loves you, Lou."

I heard nothing but silence on the other end and eventually Lou said, "She bores me. Worse than that, she wants me to leave my wife. I might have left my wife for Rebecca but not for Cindy."

I met Mr. Clarke on a Tuesday afternoon and he was congenial but abrupt. In his early fifties in a dark blue shirt and tie—he was an older version of Bennett Williams.

He had dark circles under his eyes and had a receding hairline. He looked thin behind his desk but I noticed he had a belly that, with his thin frame, made him look oddly shaped.

He held my manuscript. "Your writing is good. I like the dialogue but the prose in your narrative is way too colloquial. You can't do that kind of thing. Your narrative sounds like your characters. That's plain wrong. I'm not interested enough in your book to assign it to an editor."

He sat back in his large chair, hiding his belly, but his surly light blue eyes were clearly visible. "Bennett was not my favorite editor," he said.

He stood and put his hand out. "Good luck."

I rose in slow motion. I had trouble taking his hand. "Can you recommend me to an agent or another editor or publishing house?"

"You have talent but it's raw," he said.

"What does that mean?" I asked.

"It means you shouldn't give up your day job."

"I play poker for a living," I said with a sneer.

"That's a difficult way to pay the rent. You must be very good at it," he told me. "Stick with the poker."

I left his office, took the subway home and did a line of cocaine. I sat back in my only chair and allowed myself to dwell on the overwhelming shambles that my life was becoming.

18

I WAS EXASPERATED, FRUSTRATED AND DEJECTED. I gave up writing my novel and decided to just play poker and live life for the moment. It was too difficult to not only write but to break through the culture wall standing between me and my success as a novelist.

Despite my issues with Lou and Durrico, I knew who they were and what they were. We shared the same likes and dislikes, except my education and my need to write. However, needs fade away when they aren't met and a person learns to deal with it or crash. I wanted to continue on and, like I said, live for the moment.

Inching into the summer, Lou rented a nice house in Hampton Bays and managed to get a few weekends away from his wife, so he staked me to a couple of high-end cash poker games played in some wealthy guy's house. Each weekend when we were out there we'd either be in South Hampton, East Hampton, Bridgehampton or Montauk. The games were run by old money White Anglo-Saxon characters or wealthy Jews who didn't seem to like one another much.

The Jews made jokes about themselves and the Anglos made jokes about the Jews. Lou and I usually stood out like the goombahs invited there for laughs, danger and coke. If they made a joke about us they'd quickly apologize but we knew what they thought about us and we just accepted it.

One night a guy and his wife and kids were having dinner in a restaurant in Southampton and Lou and I and a couple of his friends I didn't know well were eating, minding our own business.

One of our guys had to pass tightly between the tables to get to the restroom and the guy with his family said something like, "Be careful."

Lou went livid. He got up and walked over to the guy and leaned in his face. I heard him say, "Shut your fucking face or I will cut out your tongue with this fork."

The guy turned white, got his check and left with his dinner only half eaten. That was the way with Lou and those guys. They'd lose their tempers and snap just like that. They despised anybody who wasn't like them.

Lou got into the round of games through a contractor who had a brother-in-law in the crowd. I never got the sense that any of the players actually liked Lou but they did like his coke. Lou gave it away at first but when he figured out one or two of the guys were hooked and wanted some for their "girl-friends" he made them pay top dollar, which he knew they could afford.

The games themselves were expensive, with a five thousand dollar buy-in. With initial investments like those, I always played slow and easy, keeping my eye on the table, trying to find the sucker, and there was always one in the game who had no right to be there. Suckers came in all types, young and old. Some played fast, loose and stupid and others were just timid.

The problem with players with big bankrolls was they were hard to bluff out. They stayed in the game waiting to hit that last winning card. There was no limit to their cash so they could always "out-bet" you and unless you had the "nuts" you'd go out. They used their big stacks to bully you out and intimidate you. The only way to beat them was to trap them and like I said before, you needed patience with that style of play.

I was on a hot streak for several weekends. Lou and I would spend weekdays in the city and weekends we'd stay at his place in Hampton Bays. His wife was conveniently taking more trips to see her parents.

We were gliding along nicely. Cards were coming our way, with players falling prey to our higher flushes and full houses as the pots got bigger and bigger all summer.

I had put away thirty thousand dollars in the bank in a savings account and figured that would be a great start to my new life. I didn't want to see past the upcoming Labor Day weekend.

* * *

THE WEATHER FORECAST PREDICTED A WARM and sunny Labor Day. Unfortunately Lou's wife stayed in the city, wanting to take him to her friend's pool club in Nassau County both Sunday and Monday, and her parents came in and wanted her close by so Lou gave me the keys to the Hampton Bays house. I drove out through heavy traffic on the Long Island Expressway and when I got to the house I felt like I was living in the lap of luxury with central air and a nice-sized swimming pool in the backyard.

Lou called and told me that there was a big game at a house right on the bay on the North Shore in a condo called Baiting Hollow. "Big money but one thing, Danny, I hear Durrico is going to be there," Lou told me.

I got quiet.

"It's a party. Figure probably sixty people, then a card game is going to break out."

"Who invited us?" I asked.

"Durrico. He just called me at the office," Lou answered.

"What about the other games we had agreed to?"

"Forget them. This one is going to be big. Some guy named Urdang and another guy named Dawson and some guy named Martini. I hear their pots get up to a hundred grand," Lou said.

I hesitated and asked, "Buy in?"

"Ten grand."

"I don't have ten grand on me. I took out the five like we figured," I told Lou.

"I know. I gave a marker to Durrico over the phone. I am staking you to the ten grand and we split whatever you win fifty–fifty."

"Okay," I said writing down the details for the game.

"Oh, by the way if Charlie invites you to a party this weekend go."

"What party?"

"I don't know. Something. I can't make it but I want you to go if he invites you."

"Why?"

"It'll help us get over the bad blood."

"And you're not going?" I asked.

"I got plans with the wife."

I hung up the phone and thought about a hundred grand in one pot. Cash. It was more than tempting and what was also exciting me was possibly seeing Nancy.

I spent that day and night alone in the house, relishing the isolation, enjoying how it gave me a sense of privacy I hadn't realized I had been craving.

I followed the directions along the dark two-lane highway that ran north and south across the island. Eventually I found a sign that read "Baiting Hollow" and saw the glowing night lights on a hill up ahead.

There was a valet who directed me to park with the other cars and I followed some couple into the condo complex. The party was on the top floor and we took the stairs. It was a different crowd for me. The women were tanned, blond and pretty in a very collegiate way. Some of the men actually wore blue blazers and ascots and white pants, despite being my age. Some of the middle-aged men were also talking loudly and I could feel the energy that a high stakes poker game brings with it.

I made my way up the stairs and into the large recreation room where cocktails and appetizers of shrimp and vegetables were being served on trays. All the men in the room were wearing sports jackets, which I had expected, so I was wearing my dark blue lightweight jacket and freshly pressed jeans and smiled at just about everyone who smiled at me.

I didn't recognize a single face and was surprised to see that there was one woman in the room. She was near fifty, well-preserved, wearing a sleek black dress covering her arms and pulled tightly against her breasts. She nodded to me and I went over and introduced myself.

"Danny," I said to her.

"Michele Urdang," she said to me.

"Here to play?" I asked.

"Oh yes I am," she said to me.

A waiter came up to me asking me my name. I gave it and he directed me to a back room. He did the same to Michele and she followed.

Once in the back room I was introduced to six other players. Five-card stud limited the players to nine. The backroom was quaint with a large felt poker table smack in the middle. I could sense that not everyone knew everyone else, though I figured half the players had some knowledge of the others.

Durrico was the second to last to walk in. He was alone. He walked right up to me and with his perpetual snicker painted on his face he took my hand and shook it. I looked right into his eyes.

"Thanks for letting me in," I said.

"Why not? You're fresh blood," Durrico said.

After another twenty minutes of small talk and waiters taking drinks, the dealer handed out place cards with numbers on them. The cards were in a basket and it was a blind pick. My number was four so I was fourth from the dealer's left. Durrico was to the right of the dealer.

The game started and as it progressed I learned the identities of the high rollers, Urdang, Martini and Dawson, and kept a watchful eye on them.

I noticed Durrico doing the same. He also kept his eyes on me.

* * *

THE GAME PLAYED OUT AS I expected. The aggressive players were letting the table know who they were. Dawson was one of them and Martini another. They raised every chance they got. Dawson seemed a little less wild but Martini would two bet and three bet on the third and fourth cards every hand.

I didn't even play a hand until nearly forty-five minutes into the game. Durrico also lay back, watching how each player handled the others and themselves.

Martini and Dawson actually had the first big confrontation. Martini was showing jacks and Dawson two diamonds. Martini was betting like he was sure he was going to buy a full house, seemingly unconcerned with Dawson's potential flush.

The pot was over thirty-five thousand by the last card, which was another diamond for Dawson, another jack for Martini. If I was either one of them I would have went out if I didn't have the full house or diamond flush but I was sure neither had either.

There is a major element of "gambling" to gambling but in a high-stakes no-limit cash game like this, you only need to win one hand to make a payday or lose one hand to walk out broke.

I was waiting to see who would bend first but neither Martini nor Dawson did. Martini bet five grand and Dawson raised ten.

The room went quiet. We were all seeing that in a game with guys with a hundred grand or more in their pockets, you weren't going to bluff yourself to a win.

Martini called, which was insane, and won the hand with the three jacks. Dawson lost the hand but made a point. You weren't going to scare him out of a pot. He would bluff with nothing more than two pair and was clearly not afraid of losing, which made him fearless in our eyes.

It was over an hour into the game when I found myself in a hand with Durrico and Urdang. I had been dealt an ace and king as my hole cards and a five up. I checked so Urdang ran the betting only showing a deuce. Durrico had a queen showing. Liking my ace and king, I called Urdang's bet and so did Durrico.

Urdang flopped a ten and my next card was a king and Durrico's was a queen. I bet and this time Urdang called but Durrico raised.

I was wondering if I was snakebit that he had trip queens since I felt that I had him beat with my kings. I looked up at Durrico and he gave me a strong "I'm here" look.

I did have Urdang behind me so that if I called I had to wonder what she would do. If she raised me, I'd lose more money or I could raise her back. I knew I might have the best hand.

I turned to her and realized I had hardly played with any women before and it was hard to read her. I found myself looking at her nicely cut long dark hair and noticing how she lowered her shoulders. She looked away from me, giving the table her best "poker face."

I folded my kings, which I knew had to be the best hand. Urdang did raise and it was another five grand. Durrico now sat back. He was beat. She had to have trips. He folded and Urdang showed her hand. She had three twos.

As he pulled in the chips Durrico said, "A pretty lady who knows how to play poker is hard to find."

"I just played my cards," she said and she was right. She also made a mistake. She shouldn't have showed us the trips. It gave the others at the table information on her.

Around three thirty I looked around the room. The players left were me, Lou, Urdang, Dawson and Martini. Dawson and Martini had the big stacks of chips in front of them. It wasn't because they were the best players at the table, I was sure Durrico was and I was a close second, but they had the big stacks because they used those stacks to bully the other players as I expected they would.

I knew Durrico and Urdang were playing like I was, waiting for the hand where they could get in deep with those two players.

Dawson was a quiet player. He looked and acted like a banker wearing a nice-pressed white shirt and open collar with a light gray summer jacket he had taken off hours ago. He wore too much cologne for me but he had thick gray hair, which he combed back giving him an "air" of confidence. From my conversation with him and other things he said at the table, I figured him for an investment banker.

Martini was big and loud with short black hair and wore an expensive short-sleeved black silk shirt with white stripes on the side. He talked through the game, not about cards but politics, money and marriage and kids. He told everyone he worked on Wall Street and lived on Staten Island.

Urdang, I learned from the little talking she did, was in real estate and owned a big house in Bridgehampton with her husband, who was in Europe on business. Eventually she got into a big face off with Dawson and we all backed away to watch.

She had a jack, ten and eight in front of her and we were all wondering if she had a queen or king or nine in the hole. She raised after the initial three cards.

Dawson had to be thinking what we were thinking—that Urdang had the straight—but he bet into it with only a pair of fives and an ace showing. Did he have the full house?

She bet everything she had, which was twenty-one thousand. Dawson paused. He looked over her cards and waited. If he had the full house he would have jumped.

Everyone could see that he *didn't* have the full house but what was incredulous was that he didn't buy her for the straight. He believed she was bluffing. So now, he had to back that up.

I looked at her and again she looked away from the table, giving us all her poker face. No one spoke. If Dawson called it would be a fifty thousand dollar and change pot.

Dawson called. Urdang went white. "You got it," she said. She had nothing. Dawson had trip fives.

Urdang kept her cool and without even saying goodbye she left the table.

Dawson pulled in his chips.

"Nice call," Durrico told him.

"Bad beat," I said.

"She's not hurting for cash," Martini said. "Her hubby's a big time attorney for an international oil company. She owns more than I'll earn in a lifetime."

I had to disagree with Durrico. It was a bad call. She made the right bluff with the right cards showing. He didn't care about the money and that was her one mistake. He'd call even with only an ace high in that spot because he had the cash and losing was only a matter of bragging rights.

Martini chimed in as usual. "Great call. How did you know the lady was bluffing?"

"I didn't," Dawson smiled.

I was right. Dumb luck was all it was.

We took a break after that hand, sipping coffee and smoking cigars out on the deck. Martini and Dawson got into a conversation with Martini's voice booming through the night air. The Long Island Sound and Connecticut were off in the dark distance. It was overcast but mild.

Durrico edged over to me. "Nancy's at the Ocean Club. She says 'hello.'"

I nodded. "Whose game is this?" I wanted to change the subject.

"Some guy rents out his condo to some of the high rollers here. It's like a commune of rich fucks," Durrico said. "She's looking good, Nancy. Nice. I bought her some nice stuff. She's educated and smart. Just like another girl I used to know.

"Yeah," I said looking right at him.

"I like these smart girls. You like them smart, too. Nancy's not as good a fuck as Rebecca though. What do you think?"

I smirked. "I don't think of rating them."

Durrico scowled. "I didn't know you like cigars," he said.

"I like cigars, champagne and cocaine," I answered.

"Slick," Durrico said under his breath.

A few minutes later a new dealer appeared and we were back to playing. It was near four a.m. when I could see Martini fading. He had been drinking scotch all night and it was starting to slow his response. Dawson was now drinking coffee and Durrico and I were drinking water.

The first hand with the new dealer brought me aces in the hole. I had to contain myself when I saw them. My first card up was an ace, giving me trips.

I did all I could to act nonchalant and saw that Dawson had a king showing, Martini had a queen and Durrico a jack. It was an odd hand to start with all that paint out in the open.

I bet five hundred and everyone called.

I was dealt a two of hearts, Dawson another king, Martini a nine of clubs and Durrico a ten.

This time I checked and Dawson bet five grand. I was thrilled. I was even happier when Martini raised to ten grand. Durrico tossed his hand and I called.

My last card was another ace giving me four aces. I was numb with excitement and disappointed that showing a pair of aces would kill the betting. Anyone who played poker knew how outrageous the odds were of getting four aces dealt to you. You'd have to have fifty-four thousand hands dealt to you to get the hand I was holding.

I waited and watched. Dawson bought another king and Martini another jack.

I did what I could in acting thoughtful, took a moment and bet five grand, expecting the others to go out. I was shocked when Dawson raised me another five grand and Martini leaned in and looked at my stack.

"What are you playing in front of you?" he asked.

In a way Martini's aggression at this moment was somewhat explainable. I was showing two aces so the odds that I had another one as a hole card was pretty high against me having it and the idea that I'd have a pair of aces as hole cards had to be nearly impossible.

I counted my chips knowing all the while I had ten grand in chips left. "Ten grand give or take a few hundred," I said.

"Well, I want to raise you fifty grand," he said loudly.

"I told you I only have ten grand in front of me," I said.

"The house rules state that there are three raises per card and a player can take a flyer on a bet," the dealer shot in.

"I'll stake you for the fifty grand," Durrico said to me.

I turned to him and gave him a long look. I did all I could not to give away that I had it but I wanted him to know that I did. "What's the vig?" I asked.

"Fifteen percent," Durrico answered.

I nodded. "Okay," I answered. Now I was sure that exchange would cool Martini and Dawson but again I was dead wrong.

Martini eyed Durrico. "You good for it?"

"I said I was," Durrico answered sharply. "My watch is worth that much." I could see Durrico was annoyed.

"Okay, so I raise fifty grand," Martini said and moved in all of his chips plus the rest in cash.

I had no idea what he had and his raise was so casual I was sure he had trip jacks, never taking me for the monster hand I was holding.

I made the call with Durrico's guarantee of the money. I was about to show my cards when Dawson, right behind me, called Martini's raise of fifty grand. I was stunned that he even considered being in the hand.

I took a long look at Dawson and he seemed supremely confident. He probably had a full boat queens over nines and never put me on four aces and I never put him on the boat. He was playing a dead hand that had to seem like a monster to him. That was the problem with poker: what you saw wasn't always what it was.

I looked at the dealer.

"Pot's good, sir," he told me.

I turned over my aces and placed them under the other two already facing up. I now had four in front of me. Dawson looked, leaned over the table, and broke out into a laugh. Martini slammed his trip jacks hard on the table realizing he was in third place. He shoved his overweight frame up out of the chair knocking it over.

I sat there, took a deep breath and leaned forward pulling the chips back to me.

Martini was livid. "I quit."

Dawson looked at him. "You came in third."

"Fuck this shit," Martini said to everyone.

Dawson looked at me. "What a hand," he said. Both he and Martini stood around a minute each taking a hit of either their coffee or booze and they both left the room.

I sat there as someone came over to me, counting out over a hundred grand in cash and laying it out in front of me. Before I pocked the money I turned to Durrico.

"Take your cut," I said to him.

Without touching a bill he counted it out, taking his stake and the flyer. He put the bills together and placed them in his jacket pocket.

I pocketed the rest and got up from the table.

"Come over to the house tomorrow. I know Nancy would like to see you," he said. "I'm having a BBQ."

"Thanks for the invite," I said and left the room.

When I got out in the open air I took a deep breath and felt the wind off the Sound blowing back my hair, caressing my face. I looked north and saw the moon trying to break through the clouds and when it did I could see the beach below. I also heard the waves crashing.

I knew I had hit the best hand I'd ever hit in my lifetime and promised myself never to play a high-stakes poker game ever again.

I got into my car and drove across the empty highway, went to the house in Hampton Bays and got into bed. The last thing on my mind before I crashed was how much I wanted to see Nancy.

19

THE OCEANSIDE CLUB WAS ON THE ocean and by three p.m. when I arrived the sky had cleared from the morning fog and it turned out to be a perfect afternoon.

The bouncers at the front door told me it was a special party and I wasn't allowed in unless I was on the guest list. I had no idea it was a party; however, my name was on the list and I went inside.

The Club itself was a rectangular structure but the appealing part of Oceanside was the individual tiny cabanas that fit eight people and came with trays for your champagne and curtains to guarantee privacy.

Once inside I saw "Happy Birthday" signs everywhere. I continued to walk through the main structure over the wooden floor and out onto the beach where a dozen cabanas, some with large colorful umbrellas, dotted the beach. Each cabana was available for those who were having private parties within the club itself. Durrico had rented out the entire club for his own private birthday party.

I wandered around, searching him out, and found him

standing strategically center stage where all the paths from the club to the private cabanas met, and right at his side with her arms around him was Nancy.

Durrico was dressed from head to toe in a white suit with one red rose on his lapel. Nancy was dressed smartly in a black skirt and light blue blouse with flowers in her hair and a little red pocketbook that matched Durrico's rose. Music played on loudspeakers but it was being drowned out by the surf and high tide. Both were barefoot.

I walked across the small portion of beach into the wind to Durrico and Nancy, holding my head up and smiling as I did.

"Happy birthday, I had no idea," I said shaking his hand.

"I wanted to keep it under wraps but this one made a big deal of it," he said gesturing to Nancy.

Despite wearing sunglasses Nancy was holding her hand over her face since the sun was drowning her in light. She reached up and quickly kissed me on the lips.

"How are you? I hear you did great last night," she said.

"He got the hand of a lifetime," Durrico chimed in but walked away when several guys came over to him wishing him a happy birthday. He sauntered down the beach laughing with them.

Alone with Nancy I felt the wind blowing my hair back in my face and saw it do it to her also.

"I never imagined you with a guy like Charlie," I said.

"Who did you imagine me with? Brian?" she asked.

"No. Me," I told her.

She was quiet. "You don't need a relationship, Danny. You have your poker and your novel. There's no room for anyone else."

"You don't believe I have feelings for you?"

"I believe you had feelings for me, but your mind was always focused on something else," she answered.

Nancy turned away and walked down toward the surf. I followed her, not caring if Durrico was watching or not.

"I never thought I'd be with a man like Charlie but I like being with him. He makes me feel safe. I don't worry about money or my future," she said.

"And you didn't feel safe with me?" I asked.

"The only other thing I can tell is that it's all about timing, Danny. When I met you I was so naïve," she said.

"We met only like six months ago," I said.

"That could be a lifetime sometimes," she answered. "Do you want a hit?" she asked.

"No."

Nancy took out a gold straw from under her blouse that she was wearing on a chain around her neck and dipped it into a vial she had in her little red pocketbook. "Charlie wants me to marry him. He said I'm the best thing that ever happened in his life."

"That's absurd," I said sharply. "A drug dealer and a schoolteacher turned drug addict. Nice."

I could feel Nancy glaring at me through the sunglasses. "He's a businessman. My parents met him and adore him. And what are you, Danny? A coke fiend and gambler?"

"I'm writing my novel. I had a publisher interested."

"You're a wannabe novelist, is what you are," she said and walked away from me.

I watched her walk down along the surf with the tide reaching her bare feet and played back in my mind what I had just said. Her words were cruel and so were mine.

Unfortunately, ex-lovers are cruel to one another sometimes and I'm not sure why. Perhaps the shared sense of failure has a lot to do with it. Probably being rejected has a lot more to do with it.

Standing on the beach I wanted to go home and be alone but I was weighted down with some painful thoughts. I thought Nancy was someone who understood me but she didn't. Perhaps she never did. She was now one of *them* more than I could ever be. I had to escape *their* world.

Just then I saw Lenny "The Roach," wearing a white sports jacket and flowing white pants, walking out of one of the cabanas with an automatic pistol in his hand, holding it down at his side.

I wanted to go over and say hello to him. It was probably just a gut reaction since I saw him so many nights at Visage but this time he had a crazed look on his face as he made his way down the beach to a crowd of men who were standing, laughing and talking with drinks in their hands in between two cabanas.

"Lenny, man, what are you doing?" a big guy with massive arms wearing a tank top shouted from behind me. I turned to look at him when I heard several gunshots go off. The automatic gunfire was drowned out by the wind, its threat sounding more like balloons going off than anything else.

I dropped to my knees in the sand and saw Lenny "The Roach" with a crazed look on his face empty his automatic into the small group of guys standing between the cabanas.

I could see splashes of blood and heard moans of pain as Lenny shuffled his feet through the sand keeping his automatic pointed at the bodies lying in front of him.

"Anthony, you fuck! You fuck! You take my fuckin' business from me? You fuck!" he said walking over to one of the motionless bodies, kicking it with his bare foot.

"Lenny, you fuckin' nutjob," a voice said behind me. Once again it was the guy with the massive arms. This time he was holding his own automatic pistol.

Lenny "The Roach" turned to the guy with the massive arms. "Fuck you too, Gino! Fuck you too!" He aimed his pistol at him.

I was right in the line of fire but I had to look with my body down in the sand. The guy with the massive arms opened fire from behind me and to my right. I saw three big blasts of red splattering across Lenny's jacket and shirt, one under his collar and two in his stomach. Lenny's head flew back, his eyes closed and his arms splayed out into the air as he fell forward into the sand.

There was pandemonium and shouts of horror coming from everyone in attendance. Despite the nearly perfect day with all the wondrous sunshine, deep blue sky and the majestic ocean only yards away, those at the party were horrified and panicked by what had just happened.

The guy with the massive arms turned to someone at his side. Still down on the sand, I could see another guy in a T-shirt and jeans, who had to be his friend.

"I have to get out of here," the guy with the massive arms said calmly to his friend. "I have to ditch this piece," was what I heard him say as he disappeared into the club.

A crowd was now surrounding the bodies. I got up and made my way toward it. As I got closer I saw Nancy standing over one of them silent, shivering. I inched closer. I had to move through moaning people hurling accusations.

I heard ambulance sirens echoing in through the wind and EMS workers pushing through the crowd and the last thing I saw before a state trooper pushed me aside was Durrico lying on his back with his mouth wide open and a large red wound in the center of his forehead.

I wanted to comfort Nancy but I didn't. I realized that I no longer mattered in her life. I turned and headed for the club and the only exit. I made my way back to my car and drove home.

* * *

"LENNY 'THE ROACH' WAS A LOOSE cannon. He was dealin' out of South Brooklyn and Durrico stabbed him in the back when he took his crew," Lou said. "Durrico thought that Lenny didn't know but someone told Lenny and 'The Roach' went nuts."

"Who do you think told him?" I asked already knowing the answer.

"Who can tell with these things?" Lou said.

"I saw the whole thing," I said. I was sitting in the back room in his office. I had gone to see him as soon as I got home to give him his cut in my big win but instead of celebration, death was the main topic of our conversation.

"Charlie was a nice guy," Lou lied. "But this time he screwed over a guy willing to die just to get even. Killed dead at his own birthday party. Who would fuckin' believe that?"

I had no idea what to say, though I figured Lou was behind Charlie getting whacked.

"Charlie got the wrong hand dealt to him at the wrong time," Lou said. "Oh well, you did good. Real good."

"Nancy was there," I said.

"Fuck her, pal. She left you for him. Wise up on that one."

"Yeah," I answered.

That night I went to Michael's for dinner and sat with him for a while. He looked more disturbed by Charlie Durrico's death than I expected.

"I don't understand the world, man. I'm really confused," he told me. "Here is Charlie having a birthday party and maybe marrying that girl Nancy and he gets killed just like that."

"I know."

Michael watched me devour my dinner of linguine and clam sauce and a large homemade salad as if I were responsible for the random act of violence that made no sense to him.

"I'm hungry, Mike," I told him.

"I told Lillian and we are so upset about the world our new baby is going to be coming into. I don't know what to do," he told me. "I can sell the business and move, maybe. Give my kid a real chance at a real life somewhere there are no guns and tough guys and drugs."

"And where is that place? Is there a place like that anywhere in the world?" I asked. "Look what happened just this week. A bomb blew up in Bologna killing close to a hundred people and maybe the mob did it."

"And her husband killed her."

"Whose husband killed who?"

"Did you hear? The playmate. Dorothy Stratten. Her husband blew her head off with a shotgun. I always liked her, Danny. She was hot, yeah, but she was pure too. Did you see that in her?"

I smirked. I had no idea what he was talking about and suddenly I felt sorry for him. "Yeah, man, don't let it all get to you."

Michael looked even more upset by what I said. He got up and walked away. After dinner I said goodbye and went home. The phone rang. It was Aunt Leigh. "There are two guys outside my house. They're sitting in their car in the driveway," she said, slurring her words. "What do these guys want, Danny?" she asked.

"I'm on the way," I told her and drove to her house.

20

I PULLED UP TO MY AUNT's house and as I parked I saw a car sitting in her driveway. They had the windows down and looked at me as I walked past them. I rang the doorbell. It was ten p.m. and most homes in the neighborhood still had their lights burning.

My aunt let me in and I could see she was drunk. She was wearing her light blue robe and it was open and she had nothing but her panties and bra on underneath. She took a step toward the driveway and I quickly pushed her back into the house.

"Fuck you!" she said to me. "I want those guys off my property."

I slammed the door shut and went to the window and looked at them again. I didn't recognize either face but I had a good idea who sent them. "Have you called anyone? Have you told anyone about what's under the shack?" I asked her.

"Of course not. What, you think I'm an idiot?" She took a sip of her vodka.

I took a deep breath. "Do you have any money left?" I asked her.

"Some, why?"

"You have to get out of here. Do you have friends anywhere out of state?" I asked.

"None."

"What about your daughter? What about Gina?"

"Fuck her," she said lighting a cigarette.

"She's in Toronto, right? Pack now."

"Are you crazy?"

I pulled her by the arm and put her face up against the window. "Look at those guys. They are hit-men and they are here to kill you."

"But why?"

"I don't know why. But I'm sure that's why they are here," I told her.

I could see my aunt doing all she could to focus, despite the vodka mixing up everything in her brain. "Your friend sent them?"

"Who else would?" I asked.

My aunt went pale. Drunk as she was, she was getting it. I grabbed the phone and called Lou at his office. I got his business message machine. "Lou, call me, it's Danny," I said and hung up. I wanted to call his house but I thought better of it. I turned back to my aunt. "Pack!"

I went through the house turning on every lamp in every room and went into the kitchen to put on a pot of coffee. I walked up to my aunt's bedroom and found her sticking everything she could in her suitcase. She stopped. She was flustered.

"I need two," she said.

"Two what?" I asked.

"Two suitcases," she answered.

"Fine. Use ten. I don't care, just pack what you need now and I'll come back and send the rest to you when you are settled in," I told her and went back upstairs, bringing my aunt a cup of coffee. "Drink it," I told her.

I went back to the front window keeping my eye on the car parked in the driveway. The two guys were just sitting there. They might have been from out of town or Staten Island or the Bronx. It didn't matter. They were sitting out in the car to make a point or worse, to grab my aunt, take her for a ride so she'd never be seen again.

When she was ready my aunt came down the stairs dressed and with her suitcases packed.

"Do you have Gina's phone number?"

"Somewhere," she said. "I haven't talked to her in years."

"That's good. I'm pretty sure Lou has no idea you have a daughter. That's where you have to go."

"Do you want me to call her now?"

"No. Once we get to the airport," I answered. "Now, do you have any cash?" I asked.

"A few bucks left," she answered.

"Under the hamper?" I asked.

"Yes."

"Get it all now. You are not coming back." I emptied my wallet of a hundred bucks and change and gave it to her. "Take this."

I took a deep breath. "Look around the house one more time. Make sure you have everything you need. Bank books, jewelry. And make sure you have your passport. Grab it and then we go right to the airport."

My aunt nodded and did what I had told her. I shut off the lamps in all the rooms and went back to the window, keeping my eye on the car and the two hit-men in it.

After a few minutes my aunt came back and nodded. "I have what I need for now."

"Give me the house keys," I told her.

She did. I walked to the door and opened it. No one in the car stirred. "Follow me to my car," I told her. As soon as she stepped out, I locked the door behind her.

I walked to the street and my aunt followed. I saw my aunt looking at the two guys. "Don't look at them," I said sharply. I reached my car door and opened it. I walked around to the back, placing her suitcases in the trunk, then opened the passenger door and she got in.

I got behind the wheel and through the rearview mirror I could see that the two hit-men continued to sit there. I started up the car and drove away.

Once on the road my aunt asked, "Are they following us?"

I could see that they were. "Yeah." I gunned it. I raced to the Southern State Parkway barreling through a red light, not worried if a cop stopped us and even hoping that they did.

Once on the Southern State I drove toward the Long Island Expressway and then toward the Grand Central and La Guardia Airport. All the while I drove I kept one eye on the rearview mirror. I didn't see their car anymore.

"Why did Lou want to whack me?" she asked.

"He figures with you gone he only has me to worry about," I answered.

Once in the airport parking lot I rushed my aunt and we made it to American Airlines. We bought her a one-way ticket to Toronto and checked her bags. It was set to take off at six a.m. so we got a bunch of coins and called Gina.

"Gina, it's your mother," I heard my aunt say as I walked away.

Once she was done with the call my aunt didn't stop talking about Gina and how much she wanted to see her grandchildren.

We then spent some time in a bar.

"I love you, you know," she kept saying. "We are blood. I could never really hurt you. Your father in heaven would never talk to me again."

"He's dead, Aunt."

"It's a figure of speech."

I gave her a quick smile.

"I say stupid things sometimes because I learned that you have to threaten people before they threaten you. It's the way of the world. Forget I ever said any bad things to you."

I gave her a nod this time.

When the bar closed at two a.m. we walked the terminal back and forth, eventually crashed and woke up when the loudspeaker announced that her flight was boarding.

I hugged my aunt goodbye and told her to send me a phone number once she had one. I watched her board and drove back to my apartment unafraid; since it was broad daylight I doubted Lou would try anything then.

"Babe" was playing on the radio as I parked my car. I saw people waiting at the bus stop. The transit strike was over. It had been for a while but I had forgotten all about it.

The Iranians still had our people and we were still being held hostage by them. Not only the embassy people they had but all of us.

Once in my apartment I locked the door and felt a lot safer. I seriously crashed this time and when I awoke I drove directly to Lou's office unannounced.

* * *

I WALKED RIGHT INTO LOU'S OFFICE and as I did I saw a few of his workers moving in and out to the backyard and truck lot and I could hear other workers maintaining his trucks and machinery.

I found Lou at this desk and I could see by the look on his face he wasn't that happy that I'd barged in on him. We were alone so I closed the door. I could see he didn't like that either. "What was last night about?" I asked.

He had a coffee and half-eaten sandwich on a wrapper in front of him. He kept quiet.

"You sent two guys to *do* my aunt? I told you she was cool."

Lou shifted in his chair, his dark murky chocolate-brown eyes focused directly on mine. Again he didn't answer me.

"Lou, talk to me."

"Where is she?" he asked.

"Gone," I answered.

"Gone where?"

"Gone someplace where she will be out of reach," I said.

Lou shifted in his chair. "What about the house?"

"What about it?"

Lou put his elbow on his large metal desk and lowered his chin on his hand. He looked away from me. "She can't sell the house. Not the way it is," he said.

"I know that. And she won't. Unless you buy it."

"Me?" Lou said.

"You can form a new company. You probably have a few already. Who will know? You buy it and demolish it," I said.

Lou listened.

"What do you think?"

"No. *You* buy it."

"Me?"

"It makes sense. You are her nephew. You buy it, take down the shack and pour two feet of thick concrete over everything," he said.

"I can't afford to buy it, let alone do what you just said," I told him.

"I can find out what that house is worth. You buy it from her and we'll get you a mortgage with Bruno. You move in."

I could see that Lou was wondering what to do with me. If he could have, I believe he would have killed me right there and then. The only thing that stopped him was that he probably didn't want to deal with getting rid of *another* body for a while.

"We should have put her in the river," he said out of nowhere as if had been thinking about it for years.

"Bodies show up in the river," I said. "Every spring they float to the top."

"We could have weighed her down. We could have taken my boat out to sea and dropped her and let the fish eat her. I think over and over about what we could have done," he said troubled and confused. "This way where she is now we got someone else involved. We got someone else who knows."

"Maybe. Maybe that was a good idea. Take her out to the ocean but who knows who might have seen us? Coast Guard might have been patrolling. It might have given Tucci a way to connect you even more. Or maybe what we did was a good idea. We know where she is and my aunt will never open her mouth," I said.

Lou sighed. "Okay," he said. "Let's get you the house and pay the taxes, do the work on it like we said and keep to our plan. That way it won't look fishy. You bought your aunt's house."

That moment I wanted to get as far away from Lou as was humanly possible. I didn't trust him and he knew it. But I was stuck. There was no place else to go. I had this life and only this life. That is how I saw things.

"Okay, we'll do it," I said.

"Great. I'll set up some games for you," he said. "Unless you want to write your novel," he smirked.

I wanted to wipe that smirk off his face but I knew that wouldn't do any good. "I want to make some real money," I told him.

"That's the plan," he said.

I nodded but I knew there was no plan. You couldn't predict the cards you were dealt. You had to play them. They were all you had. You just had to hope that you played better than the other guy and most importantly that you were lucky. And if the cards you were dealt that hand were bad, eventually that would change. You would get a new hand and a new opportunity to turn it all around.

Lou put a line of coke on the table and said, "On me."

Someday I'll take another look at my novel. Or maybe start a new one. The eighties were just beginning. I did the line.

ABOUT THE AUTHOR

Richard Vetere is the author of three novels: *Champagne and Cocaine* and *The Writers Afterlife* (both Three Rooms Press), and *The Third Miracle* (Simon & Schuster). He co-wrote the screenplay adaptation of *The Third Miracle* for the film by the same name starring Ed Harris, produced by Francis Ford Coppola, directed by Agnieszka Holland and released by Sony Pictures. His plays include *Caravaggio* and the Pulitzer-nominated *One Shot, One Kill*. He lives in New York.

Recent and Forthcoming Books from Three Rooms Press

FICTION

Meagan Brothers
Weird Girl and What's His Name

Ron Dakron
Hello Devilfish!

Michael T. Fournier
Hidden Wheel
Swing State

Janet Hamill
Tales from the Eternal Café
(Introduction by Patti Smith)

Eamon Loingsigh
Light of the Diddicoy
Exile on Bridge Street

Aram Saroyan
Still Night in L.A.

Richard Vetere
The Writers Afterlife
Champagne and Cocaine

MEMOIR & BIOGRAPHY

Nassrine Azimi and
Michel Wasserman
Last Boat to Yokohama:
The Life and Legacy of
Beate Sirota Gordon

James Carr
BAD: The Autobiography of
James Carr

Richard Katrovas
Raising Girls in Bohemia:
Meditations of an American Father;
A Memoir in Essays

Judith Malina
Full Moon Stages: Personal
Notes from 50 Years of The Living
Theatre

Stephen Spotte
My Watery Self:
Memoirs of a Marine Scientist

HUMOR

Peter Carlaftes
A Year on Facebook

PHOTOGRAPHY-MEMOIR

Mike Watt
On & Off Bass

SHORT STORY ANTHOLOGY

Dark City Lights: New York Stories
edited by Lawrence Block

Have a NYC I, II & III:
New York Short Stories;
edited by Peter Carlaftes
& Kat Georges

Crime + Music: The Sounds of Noir
edited by Jim Fusilli

Songs of My Selfie:
An Anthology of Millennial Stories
edited by Constance Renfrow

This Way to the End Times:
Classic and New Stories of
the Apocalypse
edited by Robert Silverberg

MIXED MEDIA

John S. Paul
Sign Language: A Painter's
Notebook (photography, poetry
and prose)

TRANSLATIONS

Thomas Bernhard
On Earth and in Hell
(poems of Thomas Bernhard
with English translations by
Peter Waugh)

Patrizia Gattaceca
Isula d'Anima / Soul Island
(poems by the author
in Corsican with English
translations)

César Vallejo | Gerard Malanga
Malanga Chasing Vallejo
(selected poems of César Vallejo
with English translations
and additional notes by
Gerard Malanga)

George Wallace
EOS: Abductor of Men
(selected poems of George
Wallace with Greek translations)

DADA

Maintenant: A Journal of
Contemporary Dada Writing & Art
(Annual, since 2008)

FILM & PLAYS

Israel Horovitz
My Old Lady: Complete Stage Play
and Screenplay with an Essay on
Adaptation

Peter Carlaftes
Triumph For Rent (3 Plays)
Teatrophy (3 More Plays)

POETRY COLLECTIONS

Hala Alyan
Atrium

Peter Carlaftes
DrunkYard Dog
I Fold with the Hand I Was Dealt

Thomas Fucaloro
It Starts from the Belly and Blooms
Inheriting Craziness is Like
a Soft Halo of Light

Kat Georges
Our Lady of the Hunger

Robert Gibbons
Close to the Tree

Israel Horovitz
Heaven and Other Poems

David Lawton
Sharp Blue Stream

Jane LeCroy
Signature Play

Philip Meersman
This is Belgian Chocolate

Jane Ormerod
Recreational Vehicles on Fire
Welcome to the Museum of Cattle

Lisa Panepinto
On This Borrowed Bike

George Wallace
Poppin' Johnny

Three Rooms Press | New York, NY | Current Catalog: www.threeroomspress.com
Three Rooms Press books are distributed by PGW/Perseus: www.pgw.com